up and coming author we are giving out his books for
free to show our gratitude to the fans who love the
Naga Invasion series.

www.dpoberon.com
https://www.dpoberon.com/paperbackoffer.html

VISIT

Reluctant Soldier

D. P. Oberon

ISBN: 978-0-9954075-3-4

Interior design by booknook.biz

To YOU, dear reader.
Thank you for your attention.
Thank you for your encouragement.
Thank you for the reviews.
Thank you for joining this Naga
adventure!

Table of Contents

Chapter 1

Invasion Day

New York, Central Park
28 November 2066
10:30

Ten-year-old Ben was playing in the park with his best friend Mia when the Nagas, giant snake aliens, descended from the sky in their spaceships and killed his dad right in front of his eyes.

Five minutes before that atrocity seared itself across Ben's mind forever, he heaved against the side of the swing and kicked out. He reached the top of his swing and jumped into the air. "Yippee!" he shouted as he landed on the grass in a somersault. He turned around with a flourish.

"C'mon, Mia. You can do it," Ben said.

Mia's slight hands clenched against the side of the swing. Her lower lip trembled. Her dark curls puffed into the air, revealing the chocolate-brown skin of her forehead. Her mouth opened involuntarily.

"There's nothing to be afraid of. I'll catch you," Ben said.

The two best friends always played 'swing jump' right at the end of their time in Central Park, when both their parents called them to finish up. Like both their parents did just then.

Mia's mom, Annie, and Ben's dad, Oliver, stood up from their seats under the shade of the verdant oak tree and beckoned to their children to finish playing. "Okay, kids, time to finish up," they chorused as one.

Mia kicked out with her feet, swinging her feet back and forth vigorously. As she reached the top of her swing, she jumped from the seat and yelped as she fell. She would have landed face first if Ben hadn't gotten there in time.

"Oof." The wind tore itself from Ben's mouth as Mia landed on top of him. His sneakers edged in grassy tufts and brown soil as he skidded.

Slightly dazed, he gently twisted to the side, but Mia still clung to him, shaking. The scent of sweet milk wafted into his nostrils as Mia's frizzy hair blew across his face. Inside of him, something clicked. He knew he would always have Mia's back.

"Are you okay?" Ben said.

"Look," Mia said, her finger trembling as she pointed.

A loud vibration rang across the New York cityscape. The sunny sky darkened as if somebody had tossed a blanket over the sun. Ben turned to follow Mia's terrified gaze.

Now Ben knew what put the fear into Mia.

The muscles in his neck strained as he stared up into the sky.

Only moments ago, the Manhattan skyscrapers had filled the horizon and the sun reflected against their sparkling windows. A white ferry graced the blue Hudson as it glided toward its terminal.

Now darkness obstructed the entire skyline. The sky turned from blue to a rust-orange and the blue waters blackened.

Pyramid-like spaceships filled the sky. Huge. Hundreds.

Ben couldn't even count how many there were. The spaceships stretched right across all of New York City, over the Upper West Side, Astoria, and past Williamsburg.

One of the spaceships dwarfed the others in size so much so that it made One World Trade Center look like a toy in the hand of a child. The spaceships obscured the sunlight. The vibrational noise originating from their engines caused the sky to vibrate.

Mia's mom, Annie, frowned when the grass beneath their feet darkened. Ben's dad, Oliver, got off the park bench and stared up at the sky.

One of the pyramid spaceships flew directly at them. It moved frighteningly fast.

"Ben!" "Mia!" shouted both their parents, running toward their children.

Ben grabbed Mia's hand and together they ran toward their parents. The children and parents met in the middle, forming a line as they held hands.

For several moments they stared open-mouthed at the spaceships in the sky.

"Oliver, we need to get out of here," said Annie. Mia's mom pulled at Oliver's shoulder. Her grip was so tight the whites of her knuckles could be seen.

"Okay, let's go," said Oliver. They headed toward one of the main pathways that would eventually lead them to West 96th Street bordering Central Park. That's where Ben's dad had parked the Honda Odyssey.

In the distance the sounds of cars crashing, alarms ringing, and people screaming filled the air.

Oliver, Ben, Annie, and Mia stuttered to a stop.

A pyramid spaceship hovered above them. It made a droning sound that hurt all of their ears. Ben let go of dad's hand so he could cover his ears. A huge force pressed against him, making it hard to move. An unnatural inky blackness reminiscent of octopus ink stretched out like tentacles from the spaceship. Ben's dad tripped and caught himself.

"I can't see which way to go," said Oliver, panic lacing his voice.

Annie swallowed. "Look."

The spaceship's underbelly opened like intricate origami: curved blades of a landing ramp unfurled, twisted sideways, and withdrew. A strong heat came from the spaceship and it felt to Ben like he'd put his face in front of an oven. Dark shapes hurtled out of the belly and slammed into the park's ground sending tremors to the soles of Ben's feet.

Something uncoiled from the ground and hissed. A flash of blue scales danced in the shadow. Only moments ago, the park had been covered in sunshine, and now it looked like the middle of the night. The only illumination came from the strange light of the spaceship.

"Stay close," said Oliver. He pulled on Ben's hand.

The light brown freckles on Mia's mom's face glowed. Her normally tanned face paled by fear. Sweat peppered her forehead. Her hand trembled, holding Mia's.

"Let's keep walking," said Annie. The four of them began to walk again. The only light came from the bottom of the spaceship.

The skin on Ben's neck rippled as if something in the dark watched him. He lost his footing because his dad walked too quickly, and he almost tripped, but his dad wrenched his hand. Later he would realize his shoulder had come out of its socket, but at the moment he didn't even feel the pain.

"What's that?" said his dad.

Red slitted eyes came to life in front of them. The eyes floated in black with the vague sinuous silhouette that towered over them. The red eyes got bigger as the creatures slithered forward. A glimpse of heptagonal blue scales large as a human hand came into view.

A coil of blue scales blocked their way forward.

Fear curdled Ben's stomach. Mia whimpered and cried. Her mother made cooing noises and pressed Mia's face against her side. Mia's eyes watered as the fear thick as a blanket pressed against her. She couldn't take it anymore. She ripped her hand out of her mom's and ran.

"No!" shouted Annie

Mia stopped dead in her tracks.

Another set of red eyes floated in the dark, obstructing her way forward.

Ben jumped as a resounding thump shook the entire park. The huge oak tree cracked and fell to the side as the spaceship landed on it.

The pyramid-like spaceship had an orange outline and looked like the gateway to hell. The front of it clanged open.

As Ben's eyes adjusted to the dark, he made out something slithering down the spaceship's ramp. Something big.

"Oliver, go right," urged Annie.

Ben's dad turned to the only direction left open to them and took one step and then paused.

Three pairs of slitted red eyes emerged out of the shadows. Mia gave one scream and then her head fell back, her eyes rolling in their sockets. Her mom caught her before her head hit the ground.

Each pair of red floating eyes resolved into giant blue snakes. Three huge snakes, with twenty-foot-high bodies thicker than tree trunks, slithered to the front and sides of them, forming a triangle. Each one covered an exit point. Their green scales looked so smooth that Ben wondered what it would be like to touch one.

"What do you want?" said Ben's dad. He stepped in front of Ben, Annie, and the slumped form of Mia, holding out his hands wide as if to protect them. "We are peaceful creatures."

The red eyes blinked. A dullness filled the blue snakes' gazes as if they weren't fully in control of themselves. Suddenly, the snakes shifted out of the way as another snake came down the ramp. This one was red and towered over the other snakes as if they were children. It had eyes as blue as the Hudson. The other snakes didn't have a hood. The red snake's hood flared over it, giving it a menacing appearance.

An expression of contempt flitted across the red snake's face. There was something much more intelligent in its eyes and the cunning way it measured them. A large forked tongue flickered over Ben's head and then Mia's as if tasting the children's spirit.

A warmth sensation filled Ben's shorts as he peed.

"Take these children," the red snake ordered the blue snakes.

Their parents stared at one another in shock. Annie pressed Mia tighter against her and Oliver pressed Ben tighter against himself.

Two blue snakes uncoiled themselves. One slithered toward Ben and the other toward Mia.

"No!" yelled Oliver, shoving Ben behind him.

The huge blue snake stopped in front of his dad. Oliver looked like a fly buzzing against a lion. But the snake didn't advance. It moved its head sideways to allow the red snake to see what had stopped it.

Ben knew in the depths of his bones something bad was about to happen. He wanted to pull his dad back. *Dad, come back!* he wanted to say, but the words never left his mouth.

"Imperator Kaali," said the blue snake, towering over Ben and his dad. "This human is refusing to give up its offspring."

"They are just children," pleaded Oliver. "Leave them be. You can have me, instead. Please!" He yelled at the red snake.

"You can have me too," said Annie. "Just don't touch my daughter."

The three blue snakes slithered back as if afraid of the red snake as it came through.

"Imperator Kaali doesn't barter with human scum," said the red snake, advancing. The red snake's hood flared out. Its hood glowed dully in the dark. Its mouth opened, revealing fangs longer than a rake. Sharp yellow fangs engorged in a mucus-colored venom. Its mouth revealed a purple throat surrounded by small, sharp, hooked teeth.

"Humans and their need to care for their offspring make me sick," said Imperator Kaali. "We Nagas expect our offspring to care for themselves as soon as they're born."

The red snake's wide jaws snapped open in a spitting movement. A viscous cloud puffed into the air and out of it came a sizzling venom-spit that slammed into Ben's dad.

Oliver screamed as the boiling hot venom slammed over his entire upper body. He tottered forward and crashed to his knees.

His flesh melted, the skin turning into molten wax, then mixing with the blood, veins, and bone marrow. Oliver's dying scream dribbled into a wheeze.

Where Ben's father stood now lay a puddle of blood, bones, and a rotten stench. The venom ate everything and left a white leg bone swimming in a pink goop.

Shock gripped Ben. He neared the puddle that moments ago had been his dad. Something slithery and dry wrapped around him and pulled him away.

"No!" Ben screamed. He kicked and fought with his hands, but the coils of green wrapped around him and held him so high off the ground that he felt vertigo.

His eyes caught Mia's. The green snake wrapped its tail around her limp body. She looked dead.

Chapter 2

Global Alert

Earth Defense Force - Newscast
28 October 2076

Ten years ago, the Nagas invaded Earth and wreaked havoc on our ecosystem by embedding the Nagaplex into our planet's core and over-heating our planet. Our scientists discovered then that the Nagas were terraforming Earth to suit them, but that the process would wipe humanity out.

The rise in temperature in the last ten years has quadrupled each year, resulting in dead oceans, flooded countries, and wiping out 4.5 billion people—half of the human beings who lived on this planet.

Major food crops like grain and corn have drastically been impacted. All of this forced us to impose Global Rationing and Mandatory Conscription.

A hundred million military personnel from the Earth Defense Force perished in trying to defend humanity against the Nagaplex. Each year we have launched a mission against the Nagaplex, only to be repelled.

Today marks the tenth anniversary of Operation Black Mamba, the very first offensive operation launched against the Nagaplex in which we suffered devastating losses.

The Earth Defense Force has learned much in the last ten years.

Today, we discovered that the Nagaplex is a breeding ground, and that once the Earth reaches the right temperature millions of Nagas will be spawned.

In conjunction with commemorating the heroes of Operation Black Mamba, and the impending spawning of these Nagas, which will wipe humanity out before the next twelve months are up, the Earth Defense Force has decided to execute Operation Python immediately.

It will be the last operation we launch against the Nagas.

God help us all.

ID Verifier: General Katana Bugeisha

Chapter 3

Dooms Day

High School Conscription Exams
New York, Central Park East High School
29 November 2076
13:00

B en confronted the dreaded High School Conscription Exam, HSCE, or Doomsday Paper as commonly known, along with fifty other kids from the Central Park East Graduating Class of 2076.

The next five minutes determined which division within the Earth Defense Force he would be placed in, and that would indicate how long he would live once Operation King Cobra went live in February, in three months' time. As a military school they'd already received news on the failure of Operation Python, announced only one month ago by General Katana herself.

The rest of Ben's eighteen-year-old life rested in his own sweat-soaked hands.

Bile coated his tongue because the entire jug of coffee he'd swallowed sloshed in his gut. His heart pounded, his anxiety caused his hands to break out in sweats, and his head ached. He regretted drinking the coffee.

"Concentrate, you idiot," he said to himself. His fingers were sore from all the swiping and typing he'd done to answer the previous one hundred questions as they flared to life in front of him on the tablet computer.

He looked up to see the lights from the tablets bathing the faces of his fifty classmates as they stressed over the exams. Mia's face scrunched in thought as she chewed on her stylus. Many of them, his friends, he would never see again after tomorrow.

This year would be the seventh year of universal conscription and its accompanying military curriculum. Every single high school kid from all over the planet would join the Earth Defense Force in some capacity.

Three hours into the exam and Ben knew the outcome wouldn't be what he expected. He almost wanted to press his index finger on the FINISH icon that glowed red on the upper right-hand corner of the thirty-inch tablet computer. The next section flared to life in front of him.

-Know Your Naga-

Ben's eyes widened. Finally, the section he'd been hoping for.

The page divided itself into three horizontal lines. Each section displayed a different type of Naga.

A huge red Naga rotated in three dimensions in the first line. A green Naga rotated on the second line. And a blue Naga appeared on the third line. The same bunch of questions appeared to the right of each snake.

What type of Naga? A) Viper, B) Cobra, C) Adder

What rank? A) Soldier, B) Tracker, C) General

What weapon? A) Venom shot, B) Laser eyes, C) Electroshock quill, D) Constrictor

Essay question: Q) When encountering each of these Nagas, write down a hundred-word response on how you would fight them.

Ben only had three minutes left. The virtual keyboard appeared in front of him and he began to type out his answer. The red Naga was the leader of the Nagas, Imperator Kaali; the Earth Defense Force considered the green Nagas to be some type of centurion, as they controlled lots of blue Nagas; and the blue Nagas were drone-hunters.

Earth had waged a war of attrition, until they discovered a way to effectively kill Nagas, and then they just started sending their military on suicide missions.

Ben shivered. He wanted nothing to do with the Nagas. They were unstoppable. And as far as he was concerned, mandatory conscription just meant a quicker death.

Since his father's death, Ben had spent all his time drawing, painting, writing, and getting lost in his art. It took him away from the depression of a world solely focused on war and terror. But everywhere he turned a poster of General Katana and her two huge blades stared at him. Serve your country, the posters said. Well, he would; he had no choice.

Ben thought he knew the theories to stay alive in a fight against a blue Naga. It was the only Naga species the Earth Defense Force had ever managed to kill. Nobody had yet discovered how to kill a green or red Naga.

Ben couldn't answer all the other exam questions that popped up in front of him: *Why did the Nagas invade Earth? What are the Nagas doing in their Nagaplex in the middle of the Australian desert? What would be the best way to attack the Naga-plex? How could we find out the location of the Nagas' home world?*

He jumped as the final alarm beeped on the tablet computer and the exam paper in front of him showed the final countdown of sixty seconds. Ben sat back in the seat.

He'd been so lost in his response that he'd forgotten to answer the bonus questions.

Words appeared on the screen: END-OF-EXAM. He sighed and sat back in his chair, a sinking feeling in his stomach.

"No talking until you are out of the exam hall. In three minutes the Earth Defense Force Artificial Intelligence will score your exam and assign you to a division. Your tablet computer will print out your division badge and score. You are to place this sticker on your left breast pocket and assemble in the marching yard," said Principal Bradman, as he strode down the aisle between the desks. He sported a gray navy uniform. His hair was pulled back severely into a ponytail.

Mia sat two rows left of Ben and gave him a thumb's up. Her thick frizzy hair was tied in a messy ponytail, and large glasses framed her dark eyes. She looked like a crazed scientist. Even her foundation mismatched the color of her skin and smeared itself awkwardly above her forehead. Ben frowned. He didn't know when she started wearing makeup. Only, it looked silly, as she never could find the right makeup for her shade of cocoa.

As depressed as he felt, he couldn't stop himself from smiling and nodding back at Mia. His eyes wandered two rows to the right where his girlfriend, Julie Harrington, sat drumming her fingers against the desk. She turned as if sensing his eyes on her and gave him a brief nod.

At least some things made life bearable. He had the most beautiful girlfriend in high school. He still couldn't believe it. They'd fallen in love in Ben's favorite subject: Naga-jitsu, after they'd been partnered up for some sparring. They both shared a hatred of the Nagas since Julie's uncle died serving in the Earth Defense Force's recent mission, Operation Python.

Beep. Beep. Beep. The final alarm rang and the tablet computers powered themselves off. A small slot on the upper left of the tablet printed out the student's score and a sticker showing the allocated division within the Earth Defense Force.

Ben swallowed. He watched the slot slowly print out his score. He couldn't see it, since it was printed face down. He waited until it finished printing and then reached out for it.

"Don't take the printout just yet; wait until it's printed the second part," said Principal Bradman. "That's the division sticker. Paste the division sticker against your left breast pocket. The exam score is for you, do with that what you will. The sticker will identify you clearly to the Earth Defense Force recruiters outside."

Ben breathed out. His fingers were so wet they left a streak on the printout as it began its second printing. When it finally finished, Ben reached for it and ripped it out from the slot.

He looked up and caught Mia's eyes. She held her printout in her hands; he held his. His hands shook as he turned the printout over.

Score: 22%

Division: Infantry

The printout divided itself into two halves, with a dotted line between them. The second half consisted of a sticker with the emblem of the Earth Defense Force: Earth with a shield in the middle of it and three soldiers marching below.

The average lifespan of an infantry soldier dropped into a Naga-infested landing-zone stood at sixty seconds.

Ben's hands trembled. *Don't cry,* he told himself. *Don't cry. Not in front of everyone. You've been preparing for this your entire school life.* Ever since the Naga invasion ten years ago, every single high school followed an Earth Defense Force curriculum. Military training these days started in elementary school.

Slowly, he took the sticker and pasted it onto his left breast pocket. The sticker warmed as it bonded against the shirt. It felt like a huge weight lay on him.

The other kids around him did the same. He recognized different badges: some showed a Poseidon class frigate, Navy. Others an F33-Boomerang, Air Force. But most of them showed the Army.

Principal Bradman stopped beside Mia's desk. He gasped audibly as she stuck her sticker against her left breast pocket.

Mia's badge didn't look like anyone else's. It showed a purple planet with two yellow rings forming an X.

Whispers started, with several kids pointing at Mia.

Principal Bradman and Mia just stared at one another. Mia's mouth hung open in shock. It mirrored the expression on Principal Bradman's face.

"I have a special announcement to make," said Principal Bradman, turning to face the entire exam hall. "Stand up, girl," he said to Mia. His eyes back on the students, Principal Bradman said, "In the ten years of conscription protocol worldwide we have never had a high school graduate obtain a grade that admitted them directly into the Space Defense Force." He took a deep breath and paused. Students waited with bated breath.

"Until today. I introduce you to the first student to achieve this distinction. Mia Johnson-Patel." He clapped.

Ben found himself standing up along with all fifty other students. He clapped loudly. He couldn't stop; his hands moved of their own accord.

The Space Defense Force had been only a legend. Whispers of it came and went.

Nobody knew what they did. And now, his best friend had made it in.

Mia turned around with her hand over her mouth. Her dark eyes wide in shock. Tears came down her cheeks and her hands trembled. She walked over to Ben and held out her hands.

Ben banged his hip against the side of his desk as he moved to hug her. She felt small and vulnerable in his arms. She was still tiny. Up close her badge showed the purple planet—the emblem of the Space Defense Force—divided itself into four. And then she was crying.

"Hey, it's amazing," he said. "Awesome job."

She pulled back from him and sniffed. "It means I'm going to leave Earth."

"Leave Earth?" he said, suddenly at a loss. He had spent his entire life growing up with his best friend. For a moment he couldn't understand.

It hit him like the whiplash from a Naga's tail. He wouldn't ever see Mia again for the rest of his life.

Chapter 4

Xenopsychology

Two Years Ago…

New York, Central Park East High School
13 October 2074
17:00

The last subject of the day, Xenopsychology, took place in the renovated Krumpets' Library, named after a crazy reality TV star who'd donated a billion dollars to the school.

Ben sat next to Julie and they played tic-tac-toe as the teacher talked. Julie and Ben shared the opinion that the Earth Defense Force had never successfully interrogated a Naga, so how could anyone create a valid curriculum on their psychology? Mia called it 'Pop Naga Psych.'

"How did Advanced Math go today?" Ben whispered at Julie.

"Good. I sat next to Keith and that always helps."

Ben tried hard not to frown. He didn't like Keith.

"Oh yeah? I heard he's good at math," Ben said.

Julie continued, "Mia kept raising her hand. She's an insufferable know-it-all. I can't see how you deal with her."

"It's like she's got two brains," said Ben.

"She's totally annoying."

Ben frowned. For some reason Mia and Julie didn't get along. He knew Julie didn't like Mia because she always complained about the smarter girl. He knew Mia didn't like Julie because she'd never mentioned her once, even though Ben and Julie had been dating for almost two years now.

"What about you? How's Basic Math?" Her downy eyebrows raised in appraisal. She blew a strand of overhanging yellow hair, so it edged her blue eyes.

"Not good."

"Ben, the finals are up in two years. You've got to take it seriously, otherwise you won't end up in a good posting."

"I've got time."

Julie studied him. Ben squirmed beneath the scrutiny. She reached out and held his hand. "Ben Williams, you've got to believe in yourself."

Much later he would regret not listening to this advice.

"Pay attention, you two. This is class time," said Mister Ross.

For the next thirty minutes Ben and his class got to listen to Mister Ross talking about Naga psychology.

"Eventually, it comes to the most important question, why did the Nagas invade Earth? Would anyone like to hazard a guess?" asked Mister Ross.

"To terraform our planet, obviously, like the EDF says," said Jadyn, without raising his hand. The big black kid stood six foot eight and was the school's biggest bully.

Mister Ross nodded encouragingly. "Yes, and what else?" Unlike the other teachers, he didn't make the students raise their hands.

"Everyone knows that," said Keith McAllister, another one of the know-it-alls. "That's like asking how they can speak English. We all know they have some inbuilt translation device."

Jadyn glared at Keith. "What the heck do—"

"Kids, this is important," said Mister Ross.

Ben liked the way Mister Ross diffused the situation. If he hadn't, Keith would be paying for it after class. Keith was study smart and not socially smart.

Nobody dissed Jadyn.

"Why would you invade another planet?" asked Mister Ross.

A hand shot up right at the front of the class. "But that's an anthropocentric view."

Julie splayed her fingers across her face and groaned. "Mia."

"I understand but stick with me. Why would you invade a planet?" Mister Ross asked again.

The entire class of fifty kids craned forward eagerly. Even Ben forgot about his dismal performance in Basic Math and leaned forward. Mia put up her hand again and Mister Ross nodded at her.

Mia said, "It has to be more than just what the EDF has discovered. It's conceivable that the Nagas could have destroyed us right at the very beginning. Instead, they just came here and tagged a bunch of kids, and then planted themselves right in the middle of a desert in Australia—"

All the tagged kids in the class, roughly a quarter of them, raised their hands, showing the silver bracelet on their left wrist.

When Ben and Mia were abducted that day ten years ago, that's exactly what the Nagas had done: taken the kids into their spaceships and shoved the silver bracelets on them. And then let them go. The bracelets looked like skin except they were a silver color. The Earth Defense Force couldn't work out what they were for.

"—Except the EDF discovered the Naga spaceship that landed in the middle of the Australian desert began to grow. The Nagaplex. Like *growing* every year," added Julie.

Mia ignored Julie and kept her eyes on the teacher. "I think the Nagas want to learn how to coexist with humans."

The entire class roared against this. Jadyn slapped at the table hard and rolled his eyes. His index finger made a circle around his head.

Ben stirred at that. Mia wasn't crazy; she was just super smart. Smarter than most people could even think. If they didn't live in a world with universal conscription, she would've long gone to an Ivy League college.

"That's an intriguing notion," said Mister Ross. "Well done." He rubbed his chin. "But why this planet of all planets?"

Most of the voices went quiet and hands went down. The kids could object to Mia's strange notion, but this was a difficult one.

"Maybe it has to do with us," said Mia.

Mister Ross encouraged her with an affirmative nod.

"They tagged us. Why? They didn't kill us." Mia raised her arm to show the silver bracelet that had grown to match the contours of her skin, so it lay seamlessly.

Ben remembered that day every night he went to sleep. The day his dad died.

Mia said, "The Nagas tagged a hundred and eight thousand kids ten years ago. I think they want to do something with us. And maybe this is the only planet in the universe with humans."

Julie rebutted. "There are approximately sixty-six billion planets in habitable zones. There could be loads of life out there. They could've gone to another solar system. Why would they want anything to do with us?"

Julie rubbed at her silver Naga bracelet on her left wrist. All around the world, the Nagas had tagged kids and after all the Earth Defense Force studies nobody knew why.

"There could be something special about being human," Natalie's scratchy voice spoke up. She sat in the middle of the front row and only ever spoke up in Mister Ross' class.

Natalie was the stupidest kid in their high school. She had no friends and nobody liked her. With her pale skin, limp red hair, and watery green eyes, she just gave the image of being a total weakling. And she drooled.

Jadyn bellowed, "Obviously not! The Nagas tagged a dumb bum like you!"

The class burst out laughing, but Mister Ross clapped his hands loudly, ending it. "Jadyn, a word with you later." He looked around the class. "I want to follow Natalie's line of thought. What is special about being human?"

"There's nothing special about being human," Ben interjected. "Except that we're the only ones stupid enough to drown our own planet in garbage."

"There is something special about us," said Mia. "Our brains."

"Have you met half the kids in this school?" asked Jadyn, putting his feet on the table again. "They're as dumb as can be."

Mia said, "Lazy and dumb are not mutually exclusive."

Jadyn's face screwed up as he tried to understand what 'mutually exclusive' meant. "What the heck would you know? You think you know everything," he shot back.

"Class, stay with the topic," said Mister Ross, coming to stand next to Jadyn.

"What was the topic again?" asked Jadyn.

"Why did the Nagas invade Earth?" answered Mia.

Ben shook his head. Sometimes Mia took things literally. He was about to say the topic was about what makes humans special, but he shut-up as for once in his life Jadyn actually said something interesting.

"Those snakes are already here. Who cares? I want to know what's going on with Operation Python. My brother is deployed. And we've had zero updates after the huge EDF newscast announcement."

Ben straightened his back, surprised at Jadyn. Rumors swirled in the high school about Jadyn's situation at home. He'd been close to his brother, Ben knew. The weirdest thing about the huge kid was that Jadyn had been two years ahead of Denzel, and then the school had an administrative glitch in the student's database with respect to their ages. So Denzel, who was actually the older one, was sent two years ahead and was conscripted earlier into the military and Jadyn went two years back. Ever since that happened Jadyn's bullying had been getting out of hand.

"Well, sure, we can discuss Operation Python. We've got five minutes left until the end of the day. Any ideas?" Mister Ross asked, walking around the class, his hands held out.

That's what Ben loved about Mister Ross. He didn't strictly adhere to his own class schedule. He let the kids insert their opinions.

"Aren't we meant to get an Operation Python update today? My uncle was deployed too," said Julie.

"So was my sister." "My mom." "My cousin." "My aunt." Almost the entire class had relatives deployed in Operation Python. Ben wondered what it would be like to live in a world where there was no universal conscription. War and the Nagas had been part of his curriculum his entire life.

Julie said, "My uncle is Dave Harrington, Ordnance Engineer First Class, specialist for the F33-Boomerangs. Basically, he kits them up with ordnance: weapons, fuel, ammunition, and whatever else the pilots require. We would always talk with him once a week. But then just several weeks ago the base shut down comms."

Jadyn nodded in agreement. "Yeah, same here. Could talk to my bro every week and then the EDF stopped it. Fishy stuff. What's the EDF got to hide?"

Ben said, "Yeah, but he's not a fighter pilot." Only the best pilots allowed into the Air Force got to touch the F33-Boomerang. And only the smartest kids who aced the High School Conscription Exams made it into the Air Force, and only the smartest of those made it into the fighter jet program.

Julie stared daggers at him. *What's that meant to mean?* her stare said.

"My brother said that Operation Python was meant to be like offensive reconnaissance," Jadyn said.

Mia added, "Every year since the Nagas landed in Australia, we have failed to penetrate the Nagaplex defenses. Operation Python is more than just offensive reconnaissance. There's something…experimental about it the EDF aren't telling us."

Jadyn said, "The Nagaplex has grown and grown every single year. Now it's huge. I don't understand why we don't just blow it up."

"What, you don't think the EDF has tried like a thousand times already?" Julie said.

Ben chortled into his desk by putting his hand over his forehead. He didn't see the flash of hate cross Jadyn's face. He took a deep breath and looked back up, shaking his head. Honestly, he thought Jadyn was the dumbest kid in the school and just a big bully. Only Natalie was stupider.

"Correct," said Mia. "Every bomb they've used has just backfired. The shielding above the Nagaplex repelled the bombs back into the atmosphere. The entire desert is now polluted with radiation. That radiation is held within a containment field that is failing…" Mia's voice trailed off.

Everyone kept quiet. If the containment shield failed, the radiation would eventually leak out into the cities.

"What's worrying about all this," said Julie, "is that there hasn't been any update on Operation Python for over three months. The EDF is hiding something."

The end of school bell beeped out and everyone stood up slowly. A somber mood filled the classroom.

Two years later they would find out that every single person that was part of Operation Python was dead. There was only a lone survivor.

That lone survivor was General Katana.

Chapter 5

Xenoarchitecture

Three months ago...

New York, Central Park East High School
20 August 2076
16:00

"How was Xenobio?" Ben asked Mia as they walked toward their next subject. His watch told him he needed two more hours of Naga-jitsu practice to meet his quota for the week. Two more hours left of their twelve-hour day. He wished there was a fast-forward button.

Their class schedules occasionally matched and they usually met in the middle of the courtyard to grab a quick bite at the cafeteria. Ben munched on a soy-chorizo tortilla, and Mia sipped her fresh carrot juice with ginger.

The hot afternoon sun pummeled down on the corrugated iron ceiling that covered the central walkway. Kids in their cadet uniforms walked briskly to the next class. Squat bunker classroom buildings squatted on their left and right. Occasionally, they passed an Earth Defense Force private who stood guard. Ben nodded at him.

School to Ben meant learning from an Earth Defense Force military curriculum. He found it odd when Mia's mother, Annie, told him about her pre-invasion school days. Apparently they did stuff like art, drama, and social studies. Ben wondered what it would've been like to go to school back then. He could've pursued his desire to become a writer.

"Why so pensive?" Mia asked.

"Just thinking about the military industrial complex. You know I hate all this stuff. When your mom went to school they had a library with books. We have a library with EDF weapons. I just wish I was born in a different time."

"Tell me about it. Back in my mom's day school was only six hours!"

"Six?! I've been here since 0400 hours." Ben shook his head. He hated everything about a world run by the Earth Defense Force.

Mia stopped. "Hey we'll be okay. We'll end up hunting down Imperator Kaali."

"I don't want revenge. I just want my dad back. I want to be surrounded with books, tell stories, and just live a peaceful life." Ben suffered nightmares of the red Naga wrapping his scales around his neck and squeezing until his eye popped and his brain exploded.

"Are you having a panic attack?" asked Mia.

"They're not panic attacks," Ben said annoyingly, waving her hand away. His body kept shaking.

42

"To answer your original question, Xenobiology was awesome," said Mia. "It's just frustrating because in ten years we haven't managed to catch a live Naga specimen. And the only ones we've killed are the lowest ranked drone-hunters."

"It's 'cause of their self destruct thingy they do," said Ben.

"Imagine if we captured Imperator Kaali himself?" Mia said wistfully. "I bet you I could work out a way to do that."

"Thousands of EDF soldiers have died facing Imperator Kaali." Ben's mouth felt dry. "Nobody has worked out his weakness." The leader of the Nagas appeared invulnerable.

"That's what we thought about the blue Nagas, drone-hunters. And then the EDF found a way to kill them with the M18s." She grabbed him on the shoulder and they stopped in the walkway. Other kids eyed them as they had to make their way around them. "You know, I think I may have found a way to destroy the Nagaplex."

Ben jerked his head back. "You have?"

Mia was the smartest person he knew. She was probably the smartest person in his entire high school. Later, when Ben found out how gifted her brains were, he wasn't surprised. Even back then when they were just kids in high school he sensed greatness in her.

"I kinda have this idea—"

The digital bells rang to signify the start of their next class. They both ran toward their Xenoarchitecture class.

As they ran Mia asked, "Hey, how was your Naga-jitsu? I heard you're doing pretty good."

"It was good, except I got paired with that idiot Natalie. It was painful. She doesn't know any basic moves. First time a Naga sees her she's gonna turn into Naga goop."

They descended the wide ramp and headed toward the double doors of their classroom. Kids in two-by-two formed a line. They began to walk in. Right at the back all by herself stood Natalie. She kept muttering to herself.

Ben said, "The idiot is in the same class as us? Oh no."

They were the last two to enter the classroom, but Mia stopped him on the threshold.

"Ben, go easy on Natalie," she said, grabbing his hand. "She's got troubles at home."

"Troubles?" Ben said. "Everyone's got troubles."

Mia cupped her hand around his cheek. If it were anyone else he would've shoved their hand away.

Tears began to edge Mia's eyes. She sniffed but didn't wipe them away. She stared at him. It made him feel uncomfortable.

"What's wrong? We should get into class. It's Mister Hackle," he said, feeling bad because she was crying, and anxious because nobody turned up late to Mister Hackle's class.

"Promise not to tell anyone," she said.

"Oh fine." He thumbed away her tears.

"I think Natalie's father rapes her."

༄

The Xenoarchitecture auditorium consisted of a hundred seats that fanned upward. Stairs ran up through the middle on the sides.

Julie waved at Ben as the last few students ran up the stairs and found their seats. Ben took the right stairs and grabbed a seat at the back with Julie. Mia as usual sat on the left side of the middle stairs at the front of the classroom.

"Thanks, Julie," Ben whispered, swiveling the small side desk by the side of the chair, and activating the inbuilt tablet computer.

Julie was already studying the Nagaplex 3D model that displayed itself on her tablet.

A loud whack made all the kids look down at the teacher's lectern. Mister Hackle held on to a coiled whip.

He said, "From now on, if you are more than thirty seconds late to my class I will publicly whip you. We are at war. The whole idea of adopting an EDF curriculum is to raise cadets in high schools instead of civvies. In two years time you will join the EDF as soldiers. After one year of training you could be sent to war. Time is of the essence." Another whack as he slammed the whip against the wide front desk.

Mister Hackle's black beady eyes stared up at them like a crow. A large goatee covered his sharp chin. He dressed entirely in black.

The entire class remained silent. Even Jadyn, who sat right at the back, kept his smart comments to himself.

"You pathetic children are all that's between us and the Nagas. Let me do the best I can. Hopefully you will live longer than the one-minute average lifespan of a soldier dropped into the Nagaplex. Maybe a minute and a half before their venom melts the flesh from your bones." Mister Hackle's quiet voice caused goosepimples to appear on Ben's forearms.

"But maybe, I can help you." Mister Hackle turned about suddenly and thwacked his whip against the ground. Every single student jumped at the sound.

"Look at what is in front of you. What do you see?" asked Mister Hackle.

The full class of kids stared at the 3D Nagaplex on their tablet computers. It looked like a giant oddly shaped pyramid with spines on its back. The spines stretched out like massive thorns. Each of those thorns was wider than Interstate 99. The Nagaplex on the surface was as large as the Boeing Everett Factory that covered 400,000 square meters.

Ben didn't like Mister Hackle. The teacher acted like a worse bully than Jadyn. Unlike Mister Ross, who allowed students to contribute without raising their hands, Mister Hackle picked a random victim and grilled them mercilessly.

"You," Mister Hackle said, his whip pointed at a cowering Natalie.

Natalie's fingers swiped at the 3D Nagaplex model. "A Nagaplex…that looks like it's growing in size," she answered.

"Ah finally, you've decided to use your brains instead of your stuttering. What else?" Mister Hackle limped to Natalie's chair and leaned over her.

"I…I…I…" Natalie stuttered.

"Useless." Mister Hackle switched off her tablet computer so that the 3D model completely vanished. Natalie's stricken face stared at the empty air in front of her.

For the first time in his six years of knowing her, Ben felt sorry for Natalie Sinclair. How did Mia know that about

Natalie? And why didn't anybody report it if it was true?

Mister Hackle strode up the middle of the stairs, peering left and right. His gaze cast terror in the students.

"What else do you see?" Mister Hackle's whip pointed directly at Mia.

Mia swallowed before answering. Even she feared Mister Hackle. She was the favorite of every single teacher, except for him. He hated everyone equally. Except for Jadyn. He actually liked Jadyn.

"Natalie is right; it is growing. Just not all of it," said Mia. "There are sixteen extra cones since the last time we saw this, which was last week. The pyramid-like structure hasn't grown since the first observation. Well, not to the visible—"

"I expected more from you. Disappointing." Mister Hackle tapped his black painted fingernail against Mia's desk and then abruptly switched off her tablet computer.

Mister Hackle interrogated several more students one by done. Soon half the class had their tablet computers switched off. Apparently nobody as yet had given a satisfactory answer to the question: What do you see?

"You know, it's quite disappointing. To think humanity has to rely on the likes of you to defend it. With the attitude and knowledge that you've displayed...you will all die during soldier basics."

Ben swallowed. He couldn't stop thinking about the High School Conscription Exam in three months' time. It would dictate the rest of his life. Each time he attended Mister Hackle's class he felt so useless. But why wasn't he studying? Mia and Julie had studied non-stop for over six years. He wished he could be like them.

Keith raised his hand.

"Yes, Mister McAllister. Pray tell, what have you found?" asked the teacher.

Keith, who was sitting just below Ben and Julie, typed in some commands on his tablet's virtual keyboard and the colors on the 3D model shifted. Now the Nagaplex went from being in color to black and white. With a few more toggles an intersection of the Nagaplex rendered itself. Ben didn't even know that could happen.

The second thing Ben noticed on Keith's tablet was that those sharp cones spread out like giant spikes were of a different type of texture. Keith did more typing and the image reverted back to color. Most of the spikes were blue, with an odd assortment of green spikes, and then only two huge red ones. It was almost like seeing the pyramids in the middle of a huge lush forest with a massive growth on all sides of the surfaces. Except these were Naga things.

"Finally, somebody inquisitive enough to survive," said Mister Hackle.

Keith swallowed before he spoke. "Firstly, the center structure has grown. The EDF's hypothesis is that the Nagaplex is a spaceship. Except if you look at these images, which are the old EDF pictures, and set them against a timeline of the new images—I'm looking at the closest we have from the cross section X-rays—then basically I would guess that the Nagaplex has grown downward into the earth."

Keith stood up. "May I?" He nodded to the bottom of the class where Mister

Hackle normally stooped over a large desk with a bunch of knobs on the table.

"By all means," said Mister Hackle, sitting on Keith's chair as Keith got up. It was a teacher and student swap! Ben admired the size of Keith's balls. Not many kids would do that.

"Gosh, he's audacious," said Julie.

Ben felt a twinge of jealousy as his girlfriend stared with wide eyes at Keith.

Keith sat behind the big table and pressed a few buttons on the table's built-in keyboard. Immediately, the remaining tablet computers that were still on turned off and all the lights in the room dimmed.

A huge Nagaplex hologram flared to life and rotated in the middle of the classroom. Now all the kids could see what Keith was seeing.

"This was the Nagaplex when it first landed," said Keith. "Pay attention to the spaceship itself." The pyramid shaped spaceship sat in the middle of the Australian desert. It was the largest spaceship out of all the Naga spaceships that had come to Earth on Invasion Day. It had golden sides, with each side consisting of three hexagon doorways lining up in the middle.

"Year one," said Keith, and the display showed the Nagaplex one year later. "Year two. Year three." Keith took a deep breath. "Now watch closely. This is just one day out of an entire year's footage this year."

A huge gap in the sand appeared below the Nagaplex. The huge spike-like structures had already grown out, the semblance of it being a Naga spaceship had truly gone, and it now looked like the Nagaplex.

But that wasn't all.

The huge gap below the base of the pyramid stretched all the way down. The hexagonal doorways stretched down for twelve stories before disappearing into the Earth.

"This means the Nagaplex stretches down into the earth. Below the pyramid is a square-shaped structure that goes into the depths. Possibly there is some type of umbilical connecting the Nagaplex to the Earth's core. Which may have something to do with the accelerated global warming since Invasion Day."

A hollow clap sounded and everyone's eyes turned to Mister Hackle, who stood up.

"Memorize the Nagaplex," he said. "You may be the first humans to get inside of it."

If only Ben knew how prophetic Mister Hackles words were, he might have studied the model a little deeper.

ʓ

Device: EDF Provisioned High School Tablet Computer

Owner: Julie Harrington

Application: iChat

Alert: [COMINT] AI censor detected contextual keyword. Escalated to EDF Intelligence Analyst Noah Harper for IMMEDIATE REVIEW.

Date/timestamp: 20-08-2076 03:00

START/

Julie: Hey babe, are you awake?

Ben: Yeah, can't sleep. Having nightmares.

Julie: Oh poor baby. Well just imagine I'm there and we're spooning.

Ben: Haha

Julie: Remember how we were studying the Nagaplex earlier today?

Ben: Yeah?

Julie: I've found something!

Ben: ???

Julie: Might be possible to land right inside the Nagaplex itself.

Ben: Seriously? Why haven't the EDF or the SDF found that out?

Julie: It's not possible to get through without some serious flying. Probably if you took a group of pilots, maybe two F33s and one G15. The two fighters could provide cover for the attack helicopter.

Ben: The EDF has F33 pilots. Why haven't they done it?

Julie: I ran through a simulation. Six F33 pilots died and the G15 didn't get to land.

Been: Sheezus.

Julie: Each F33 costs five hundred million...

Ben: ...and the EDF just hasn't been that desperate yet.

Julie: *snap*

/END

Chapter 6

Universal Conscription

Present Day...

Universal Conscription Week
New York, Central Park High School
29 November 2076
16:00

Geneal Katana stood on top of a large circular podium in the courtyard. The hero of Operation Python dressed completely in black. The only color came from the array of ribbons on her chest pocket showing all the military campaigns she'd been involved with. Every single school kid completing the Earth Defense Force curriculum knew about her Purple Heart and Medal of Honor.

General Katana's sleeveless shirt bared her arms from the shoulders down. Ten black lines for each Naga she'd killed marked biceps large enough to lift a car. Spiky silver hair fringed over a livid scar that went between the General's forehead, across her nose, and down to the right of her chin. Her left eye clicked and zoomed as she stared at the students. A black eye-patch covered her right eye. Two katana hilts jutted out from her back.

Ben felt her gaze like hot lasers as she stared at the students. A tiny pair of silver katanas glinted on her lapels. That was the badge of the Black Berets, the Earth Defense Force's most elite regiment.

Ben couldn't believe that he now stood in front of the newest leader of the Earth Defense Force, along with the rest of his school. Rumor had it that the General had chosen to deliver the graduation speech at Central Park East High because of Mia's astonishing achievements. Only the schools with the best results ever got General Katana for the graduation speech.

Dozens of Earth Defense Force soldiers arrayed themselves around the courtyard. Their hands held black M18 rifles and their steely gaze seemed to stare at him. Ben felt trapped. A seizing sensation choked him. *This is it*, he thought. *My life is about to end in the military.* He shivered in fear.

Mia stood next to him. She reached out to hold his hand but he shook his head. Nobody else held hands.

General Katana spoke. "The EDF launched Operation Python four months ago after five years of planning. The goal was simple: destroy the Nagaplex. To do that we needed to terminate the shield over the Nagaplex and then infiltrate it to destroy their land-to-air missiles. This would allow the EDF's F33-Boomerangs to drop their nukes. Even though we managed to destroy the shield and most of their land-to-air missiles, we failed. Catastrophically.

"I am the sole survivor of Operation Python. The first time we fought against the Nagas, ten years ago, when they invaded Earth, they slaughtered us like ants." Her deep voice pulled at the audience like gravity. "This time we managed to go one step further.

"After spending over half our infantry resources in destroying the shield barrier, my squad was decimated. I managed to infiltrate the Nagaplex by myself. There I came face to face with the Naga they call Imperator Kaali. The Red Naga, as he is infamously known. We fought, me with my katana, and him with his killer venom and jaws that would rip holes in concrete as if it were toffee. I aimed a killing cut across his hood and he spat venom at me." Her black fingernail traced down the scar bifurcating half her face. *That's how she lost the eye*, Ben realized.

"The venom burned across my body. The agony of a thousand fire blades tore across my skin. Imperator Kaali squeezed me with his snake body and began to crush me. That's when I thought I would die. That's when I thought it would all be over. He snapped my spinal column and left me for dead."

The long black jacket that hung down to her legs flared open as she stomped her left foot and then right foot outward. Two concave-shaped, steel-gray robotic legs curved downward and ended in several large claws. It reminded Ben of a T-Rex.

"It took me five days to drag myself out of the Nagaplex back to our secret landing zone, where I radioed for evacuation." She paused. She held her left hand out and a tiny round robot jumped from her palm into the air.

The robot opened one cloudy eye and light shot out of it, turning into a 3D image that projected out over the air.

The hazy scene showed an underground with little light. Large eggs hung from sacks in the ceiling. The camera panned and revealed dozens of rows of eggs; it zoomed out and the entire enormous cavern filled itself with eggs stretching as far as the eye could see.

Thousands of them.

The robot switched its display off, and the light sucked itself back into its cloudy eye. It floated into the air and returned to General Katana's palm.

"What I found that day was this: that the Nagaplex isn't just for them to accelerate the Earth's temperature for the eventual arrival of more Nagas, but it is an active nesting site. The other Nagas are already here. It takes ten years for a Naga egg to hatch. Our estimates indicate those Nagas will hatch by the first of March next year. Earth will be run over by the Nagas. Your families will not survive. Nobody will survive."

Suddenly, she reached behind her back and ripped a katana from its sheath. It made a ringing sound in the air, leaving a clear note hovering in Ben's ear.

And as bad as Ben wanted to get away from his destiny, as bad as he didn't want to end up in the grunts to become Naga meat, as bad as he didn't want to leave the comforts of his home, some part of him stirred at that sight.

"Operation King Cobra: in three months I will lead us back into the Nagaplex. Our goal is simple. To annihilate the Nagaplex. To rid the Earth of the Nagas' foul presence. We have ten generations of military history from our confrontations with the Nagas. The Space Defense Force has come up with newer technology. Every. Single. Person. Counts. All of you here today will be in some way, shape, or form part of that force I lead. Most of you in a support role. Welcome, my sisters and brothers. Welcome to the fight." She bellowed, "Operation King Cobra!"

General Katana shouted the cry three times.

Ben didn't join until the last cry, when all his friends around him shouted. He couldn't help but think by saying those words he gave his life to General Katana, like he was making a personal vow to her.

Mia frowned as she looked down at the ground. She whispered to herself, "Surely that's not possible. That means the General intends to train us for three months only before we face the Nagas. The average soldier in Operation Black Mamba had five years of military training."

Ben couldn't hear as the chanting from the others turned into a roar of defiance. "Operation King Cobra!"

After General Katana's graduation speech, Ben's mood went into a dark spiral. When she was there the General was like the sun, and when she left it was as if she took the sun away with her.

Ben was in shock. His entire future had changed today. He couldn't help but feel death loomed over him. And even when Mia squealed in delight and hugged him, he couldn't clear his mind away.

Ben disengaged himself from Mia and smiled at her. "Well done. Go home and tell your mom," he said.

"When are you coming? Let's go out and celebrate," she said, holding his hand. A big goofy grin split her face.

"I'm going with Julie," Ben said, feeling suddenly annoyed at her.

"Oh," said Mia. "Well, will you be back at night? We could have a tea then."

"Mia, just leave me alone," he said.

Ben headed through the throng of high school kids all wearing their Earth Defense Force cadet uniforms with their digitized gray and white panels optimized for urban warfare. Schools had standardized a universal uniform after Invasion Day. Their clothes were completely functional. Apparently, the uniforms they would get at the Earth Defense Force weren't too much different.

Julie stood in the middle of a crowd of boys. Her blonde hair in a Dutch braid cascaded over her neck in intricate plaits. Her eyes, the color of the Hudson at twelve o'clock, crinkled against the harsh sun. Her mouth curved up in a smile as she joked with somebody. Julie's silver bracelet looked stylish, like something a fashion model wore, instead of a device snapped-on by aliens.

"Well done, Julie," said Keith McAllister, pushing in from the side. Ben stumbled to the side and almost would've pushed him back if Julie hadn't been hugging Keith.

"Oooh, you made it into the Air Force too," said Julie, holding out one hand to give Keith a cuddle, making a cooing noise as she stared at the badge on Keith's uniform.

"Yee-Hah! Can't wait. We're all in the Air Force. Well done everyone!" Keith roared and turned, high-fiving everyone in the circle.

With a sudden chagrin Ben realized Julie's entire group of friends wore badges depicting the F33-Boomerang. They'd all made it into the Air Force.

Keith came to a stop when he spotted Ben. "Oh hey, lover boy."

"Julie, well done," Ben said, giving his girlfriend a kiss on the lips, but she turned at the last moment and he brushed her cheeks. He stood near her but she kept a distance.

Julie gave him a quick pat on the back as he appraised her.

"What did you get?" she asked, her eyes settling on the badge on his left breast pocket.

"Oooh!" said Keith. "We have a grunt here, ladies and gentlemen. Naga meat! Don't worry, we'll protect!"

All the other boys around Keith and Julie laughed. Only Julie didn't laugh. Her lower lip trembled. Her hand wiped at her mouth as she always did when upset. Her finger traced Ben's badge: Earth with a shield in the middle of it and three soldiers marching below.

Her touch felt like a blowtorch. Ben flinched away. A tear appeared at the corner of her eye, and instead of him reaching out to hug her it was Keith.

"Why don't you come back later," said Keith.

"Why don't you back the fuck off," said Ben. The rage flared up in him abruptly. It was always like that, lurking in the back, ready to flare. It scared him.

"You back the—" said Keith, but Julie gently tugged him away.

"Let's go, we need to talk," said Julie, reaching out and grabbing Ben's hand.

Her cool fingers drained his anger away. He followed her and felt his face heat up as the others around them laughed.

The courtyard began to empty out as the kids were allowed to head home to prepare for tonight's graduation party. Tomorrow would be Family Day, the last time they would get to spend with their families before being shipped off to war.

Ben swallowed as he watched the courtyard empty out. It was like watching parts of himself be chopped out and shipped away. How many of his friends would he see again? How many would die in the oncoming war against the Nagas?

"I'm sorry," he said, when Julie stopped walking.

"Why didn't you try harder?" she said, her hands gently beating at his chest. "Dammit, you're smarter than this, Ben Williams."

A thickness filled Ben's throat. Frustration at himself, anger at Keith, and anger at the injustice of his situation. Sadness and despair.

"I don't know," he answered.

"Because you were too damn lazy. I told you to study."

"I tried."

"That bullshit two hours of study mixed with hours of you zoning out on the net isn't trying."

"Let's just celebrate your achievement. You made it. That's good, right?" he said.

Her mouth closed mid tirade. Those beautiful soft lips. Ben jerked forward and pressed his lips against hers. For a moment she resisted. She gave in briefly and then pushed him back, shaking her head.

"What?"

"Ben, you've got to change."

"I'll come pick you up at eight-thirty?" he said, hearing her words but not listening to them. They'd had this conversation before.

"No, I'll meet you there."

"Sure?"

"Yeah."

Chapter 7

Heart Break High

High School Graduation
New York, Central Park High School
29 November 2076
19:00

'Sweet Georgia Brown' tromboned into the air. Brightly colored American flags snapped from tall bronze flagpoles. The Earth Defense Force triangular pennants connected themselves in a string from one flagpole to the other. A huge banner reading 'Central Park East

High School Class of 2076' fluttered just above the entrance. The music came from beyond in the central courtyard, temporarily converted into an open-air dance hall.

Ben imagined the same scene happening in high schools all over the world. In two days' time he would meet all those other kids. Anticipation and nerves flared within him.

"You want to come and dance—join us?" Mia asked, as they passed under the banner.

"No, you guys go ahead," he said.

"Let's go, Iggy!" Mia pulled on her date's hand and ran toward the dance floor. Ignatius, Mia's date, another super geek, smiled and nodded at Ben. The kid had gotten into the Air Force and directly into the Advanced Avionics program. Ben heard all about it during the car ride.

They were running an hour late because Mia wanted to get laser eye surgery from the local clinic. She'd never bothered until now but it was mandatory for anyone being admitted into the Earth Defense Force, or even the Space Defense Force.

Blue, red, and white lights floated up in the air carried by drones. They formed different patterns in the night sky. It was always hot since the Nagaplex accelerated global warming. Ben wiped at the sweat on his brow and undid his tuxedo.

The Radical Rascals, a live band consisting of kids from the school, played music. Ben only knew two members, Andy and Matt. He didn't know the other two girls. They were getting the crowd going.

Ben walked around the courtyard, his eyes peering into crowds of kids, looking for Julie's golden hair. He chewed his lower lip and shook his head. Where was she? He headed toward the drinks where a lot of kids hung around. The Earth Defense Force permitted alcohol consumption at graduation. Mia's theory was that they wanted kids to forget what would soon happen to them. But it would be the last time he could drink alcohol. It was completely banned once recruited into the Earth Defense Force.

"Hello Ben, where is your girlfriend?" asked the redheaded girl. She wore her hair in a skull braid, showing the left of her skull, and the braids cascaded down on the right side of her face. Her cheekbones dotted with perspiration added an alluring glow.

"Natalie?" he said, not quite believing the transformation.

"I've been dancing. It's so much fun," she said. "I'm tired though." The smell of vodka exuded from her breath.

Ben grabbed a twenty-five-ounce bottle of Absolut America from an ice slushed repurposed ammunition crate. He clinked bottles with Natalie.

"To the Nagas hopefully annihilating themselves and the war finishing before we even get admitted," he half joked.

Natalie blinked abruptly as she felt the vibration from the clink on the bottle she held. Her oddly shaped gray eyes found his. "I can't wait to go. I've been dreaming about this for ten years."

Ben blinked and almost coughed as the rough vodka slid down his throat. It burned like a thousand lit matches in his stomach.

He had never ever heard somebody eager to join the Earth Defense Force. Maybe Natalie didn't understand?

He said, "We're going to be on the ground fighting giant snakes that are mostly likely going to burn us alive with their venom." Natalie's score had been only a percentage above his. They were both going to infantry.

Natalie smiled. He'd never seen her smile. It terrified him.

"I'd take that over what happens to me at home," she said. A tear slid down her eye and she rubbed at it. Her hand shook as she downed the bottle in large gulps. "Oh, I remember I saw Julie and Keith near Xenopsych."

Ben remembered what Mia once told him, that Natalie's dad raped his own daughter. The redhead cut a lone figure as she as she headed to the dance floor.

"Hey, Natalie," he called out.

She stopped, turned around, her eyebrows curved up.

"On Family Day, come have dinner at my house. Mia will be there," he said. Never in a million years had he thought he would ever invite the class idiot to his home.

Natalie swallowed as tears slid down her cheeks. She shook her head. "I can't. Dad will…" She turned and fled onto the dance floor, pushing people aside, running away.

Ben shook his head. Stared at the glistening Absolut America he held in his hand and drained it. The cold crisp vodka tasted like vomit.

He grabbed a six-pack of Miller from the ammo crate before heading to the Xenopsych classrooms. He needed to wipe away that look of stark terror that etched itself onto Natalie's face when she said the word 'Dad.'

The Radical Rascals started to play 'U Can't Touch This.'

Ben passed many sweaty faces. Girls he would have thought were beautiful before he'd met Julie. Now all his eyes could do was search for her. He did admit to himself that everyone looked great tonight.

He stopped when he passed Mia. She danced wildly, swinging her hands around from side to side. Something caught in his throat.

74

Before long he'd cut across the entire dance floor and ended up at the other end.

A long white table with iced bottles of beer and soy-meat skewers greeted him. He realized with a surprise that he'd drunk the entire six-pack as he made his way across the dance floor. He lobbed the empty bottles like he was shooting a basketball, and they clunked into trash.

He downed his seventh beer as he chewed on a soy-meat skewer. Anxiety flared through him, causing his heart to palpitate. All he could remember was reaching for the printout and seeing his score. He downed the eighth bottle and reached for a ninth. He needed to get rid of the anxiety.

He turned to reach for a few more skewers when out of the corner of his eye he caught the silhouette of a guy and girl heading past the trees toward the shadowy end of the Xenopsych classrooms.

Something about the silhouette reminded him of Julie. Before padding after the couple, he downed his tenth beer.

He stumbled after them. The world swaying in his vision. He looked at a magically-appeared eleventh bottle of beer in his hand. He gulped it.

His head pounded as he ran along the grass, heading toward the shadowy end of the courtyard where the squat Xenopsychology building sat. Here the American flag interspersed itself with the Earth Defense Force flag. He caught up to the couple and spotted a glimpse of blond hair. His heartbeat quickened.

The couple turned the corner and went down a set of stairs that edged the Xenopsychology classroom.

Ben followed.

Something prickled the back of his neck. A sensation twanged in his gut. Later he would trust his gut completely when he felt that twinge.

A cold wind whipped at him. Overhead the crescent moon cradled the full moon. The dark sky emptied itself of stars.

Giggling up ahead. A fern with ticklish fronds pushed against Ben's face as he peered at the two graduates who sat down against a steel bench.

The saliva in his mouth dried. His hand trembled by his side. The beer bottle almost slipped from his fingers.

Julie looked gorgeous in her slender black dress. Her left wrist sported a glittering crystal bracelet. Her hair was gold tonight and tied back into an elaborate braid that showed off her oval-shaped face. Long slender hands lay stretched out against one knee. Her legs crossed, revealing the gentle curve of a shapely thigh. An overturned champagne glass slumped on her right. Rose-scented perfume wafted into the air.

"I knew you would do it," said Keith McAllister. He wore a white shirt with a blue tie. His black jacket lay on the ground as a makeshift blanket for Julie to sit on. He patted Julie's knee and his hand stayed there. "F33-Boomerang fighter pilot right here! Do you know how hard it is to do that?"

Julie laughed. "We both did it." She held out her hand and they high-fived. She said, "I dreamt of being a pilot since I was eight. My father and uncle both died in the Air Force fighting Nagas. I will avenge them. I studied so hard for this."

"I'm sorry to hear about that. I never knew." Keith squeezed her knee. "Thanks for encouraging me. You were the one that got us into those F33 sims. Without those I doubt we would've scored as high."

"It's such a relief," said Julie. "I just…"

"What is it?" said Keith.

"I wish Ben tried harder," she said.

"You're kidding me? He sleepwalked his entire high school life. I've known him from his junior year when he was only twelve. He showed zero interest in anything to do with school."

Ben bristled. A heat suffused his chest and face. His teeth grinded against one another. Sleepwalking? He just hated most of the subjects. They were stupid and didn't make much sense.

"This is military curriculum. He likes to draw, write, and be creative. The current system doesn't allow for that," said Julie.

Keith snickered. "The Nagas killed his dad and all he wants to do is draw?"

Julie sighed. "I think he's still depressed from losing his dad."

Keith snorted. "What, like ten years ago? Jules, we all lost things ten years ago. You just told me you lost your uncle and dad. I lost my mom."

A tear slid down Julie's cheek. "Ben's a good kid. He's just lost."

Keith thumbed away the tear that slid down her cheek and kissed her suddenly.

"I—" She pushed him away.

"You deserve so much better, Julie." He gently cupped he chin and stared into her eyes. "You're beautiful, talented, intelligent."

Keith leaned in and their lips meant. This time Julie didn't resist. The first kiss was tentative. Julie's hand pressed against Keith's cheeks, and they kissed deeper and much longer this time.

"You've got to tell him it's over," Keith whispered.

Julie draped her head against Keith's shoulder. "I'm so scared for him. He's going to die in the—"

"We could all die, Jules. Don't worry about him. He can look after himself."

Ben's anger bloomed like a bomb. He wished he could spit venom like a Naga. He wanted Keith to smolder and burn.

Ben stepped forward, his hand clenching the beer bottle. "Fuck you!" he screamed. His hand threw the bottle at Keith. He couldn't even feel his hand. It moved as if disconnected from his body.

The bottle rotated through the air and smacked the side of Keith's head. A red gash appeared on his forehead.

Ben leaped at him.

Keith's eyes widened in shock. Julie screamed. Ben's hand came up and then down. Up and down. Pummeling Keith.

Keith kicked out and Ben staggered back but that didn't stop him. He jumped at Keith.

"Screw you!" Ben roared. All the rage, the unfairness of conscription, his self-loathing of the fact he hadn't tried hard for a single year in high school, it all came out right then.

The smell hit him first. Julie's perfume. Her hand stretching across to protect Keith. Her mouth opened in a scream. All of it in slow motion until her scream shattered his trance and everything crashed.

He stared at his hands. Keith's screaming face. The bloodied left eye. A puddle of blood pooled against the ground.

Ben stared at Keith's eyeball in his right hand.

Chapter 8

Secret Recording

Secretly recorded conversation between the local Earth Defense Force military police and Mister Slash Hackle (a teacher at Central Park East High School).

"Kids fight."

"He ripped the boy's eye out."

"So what? He's going to be infantry. His aggression will serve him."

"He's damaged. You're not going to reprimand him?"

"I've been watching him since he was a kid. There is a rage in him. He has potential to be a true berserker."

"Berserker? These kids are still my charge. I have a duty of care to keep them safe. They are not yours yet. I want you to take action."

"If it happens again, we'll throw him into a civvy jail for a night. Let him stew in his juices. He'll be with us in a day. After that you won't have to worry about him anymore."

"Family Day is tomorrow. He'll do something stupid."

"They all do. For many it's their last civvy day ever."

Chapter 9

Family Day

New York, Chinatown
30 November 2076
20:00

The Nagas' sizzling spit seared the air and Ben didn't step away in time. He watched as the computer arcade game's camera went from first person to third person, showing his avatar's body burning from the vitriol. The haptic armor Ben wore vibrated and huge words appeared in a red hologram: 'Player 1: Game Over.'

Ben stepped out from the play area, took off the armor, and shoved it onto the rack. A line of kids formed in front of 'Naga Infestation,' the first-person shooter game. He used to be good at that game, but now he didn't last five minutes.

The graduation party last night had turned out to be a nightmare. He'd broken up with Julie, gotten drunk, and Mister Hackle had apprehended him and reported his assault on Keith to the Earth Defense Force. Strangely, Mister Hackle had let him go after an hour of stewing in his office.

Tonight he and Mia had come to the arcade while Mia's mom, Annie, waited in line at Pizza Palace. Ben, who was normally a good player, kept getting killed. He walked around Old School Retro Arcade, staring over the shoulders of other kids at the games they played. The smell of oil, the hiss of pneumatic pistons, and flashing lights normally comforted him, but tonight he felt irritated.

A familiar voice made Ben turn around.

"I won a teddy," said Julie, coming up from behind Keith and wrapping her arms around him.

Keith laughed as he grabbed the brown teddy bear. It had a heart on its belly with 'I Love You' in pink.

"Why are you shivering? You want my jacket?" Keith asked.

"Let's get out of here," said Julie, who'd just noticed Ben staring at them from the other end of the arcade.

"Sure babe," Keith said, finally noticing Ben too. He wore an eye-patch since his new bionic eye required a twenty-four-hour bedding in and wouldn't be fully active until tomorrow morning.

Shame heated Ben's face and he quickly turned away. He didn't want to get in trouble. All of last night he hadn't slept. The nightmare of Imperator Kaali killing his dad woke him up in a sweat. Then he'd stayed up all night waiting for a knock on the front door from the military police. But there had been no knock.

Family Day, an Earth-wide public holiday, meant the last time that families got to spend with the newly minted recruits before they were shipped off to war.

Ben's face felt hot and he wanted to take his jacket off. His heart pounded. He walked toward the exit but stopped as a large group of kids gathered around watching Mia play 'Nagaplex Invaders,' a complicated real-time strategy game.

Ben joined the group of kids to see what the big deal was. It turned out Mia had made it to the final mission. It piqued his interest; nobody had ever made it to the last stage of that game. It was the toughest strategy game of all time. More like a simulation strategy because it was so real. The arcade version only gave the player one life.

Mia's hundreds of Earth Defense Force soldiers in their army fatigues surrounded the huge Nagaplex that jutted out from the middle of the desert. The last round began with a ring of the bells.

Immediately, a hundred blue Nagas slithered out from the Nagaplex. Mia wore a neural helmet that sent commands directly from her brain to her units on the big display. She arranged her units in a semi-circle, but when the blue

Nagas came close she moved them away and brought out her artillery. The Nagas turned to splatters of blood.

Ben watched in amazement. Nobody had gotten this close to the end. Eventually, the green Nagas came out and Mia defeated them using a strategy Ben had never seen before. All the kids around Mia whooped and hollered.

Mia's face was covered in sweat and her frizzy hair clung to her cheeks. Her lips moved and her fingers twitched. Only the color from the screen flashed against her irises. The real world was dead to her.

The last round started. Mia only had six troops left, one F33-Boomerang fighter jet, and a missile silo. All the kids around her kept quiet as the words 'Final Round' flashed in front of them. A loud drum-beat came from the speakers and made the floor of the arcade thrum beneath the kids' feet.

On the large holographic display, a huge red Naga slithered out of the Naga-plex. 'Imperator Kaali' flashed the words above the alien snake. The red Naga moved twice as fast as the other Nagas.

Mia's F33-Boomerang blazed its gauss-cannons. The nozzles flashed and covered Imperator Kaali in smoke. She didn't wait to see what happened, but immediately moved in three of her troops. The smoke cleared and an unscratched Imperator Kaali slithered out. His mouth spat venom that instantly melted Mia's troops into puddles of blood.

The F33-Boomerang was the last piece Mia had. She directed it to the middle and had to move it several times as Imperator Kaali's eyes shot out lasers.

Then Mia did something that Ben had never seen other kids do before when playing Nagaplex Invaders. She self-destructed the F33-Boomerange right over the Naga.

But something happened, and the game's screen went blank and then blue. 'Report Crash Information 0X00ADBC' displayed itself before the game reset. All the kids groaned in despair as Ben pressed himself through the crowd and neared Mia.

Gently, he reached out and took off the neural helmet. It was caked in sweat.

Mia's face stared at his. On impulse he kissed her on the cheek. "Wake up, zombie. That was a top score."

"It crashed! I should've won," Mia said.

"Don't worry. You did well," Ben said. "I mean, it's not as if anybody has found a way to kill Imperator Kaali."

Mia looked good in her green skirt that showed her legs and her fluffy green jumper and green hair band. He noticed for the first time, ever since they'd been best friends when they were eight, that his close friend would be a gorgeous woman one day. It caught him unawares and he just stared.

"Is something in my hair again?" she asked.

"No." He laughed as he pulled on her hand, taking her outside. "Let's get out of here."

"Where's Julie?" Mia asked.

"Oh," he said, letting go of her hand. "In there somewhere." He nodded toward the back of the arcade. "She was talking to Keith, last I saw." Ben didn't notice Mia's expression dip and then smooth out when he said that.

"Mom just texted. She's got a seat in Pizza Palace, woohoo!" Mia's infectious laughter pulled Ben out of his dreary mood.

"Good. I'm starved. Let's get out of here."

A slight drizzle fell over New York City. The sidewalk was packed with families and their newly minted Earth Defense Force recruits. Food vendors in their vans sold soy hot-dogs, and one van, 'Mama's Jamaican Kitchen,' had a long line of people. A woman with dark frizzy hair and a colorful beanie smiled from the van's window as she greeted her customers and dished out food in white foam containers.

A hover tram zoomed by and stopped. Its doors swished open and a group of loud-mouthed youth stepped out. A huge hologram advertisement showed fried noddle's twirling in the air flashed above the tram: 'Family Day Special: 50% off for EDF recruits and families only at Noodle King.'

"Been a while since I've seen New York City like this," Ben said.

"Hey if you ever want to talk—"

"Well, well, well. There's Benny doll," boomed a voice. It belonged to a huge black kid wearing a hoodie. The hoodie fell back to reveal an immaculately sloped high-top afro that gave Jadyn a cool look. His puffy lips sported black bruises as if he'd been in a fight. An e-cigar dangled out between a gap in his teeth.

Mia stilled immediately upon seeing Jadyn. He had that effect on lots of people.

"Hey," said Ben.

"Can't believe you only got twenty-two percent on your exams. Heck, I got twenty-five percent. I beat you by three. How come you so dumb?" Jadyn walked right up to Ben and stared down at him. His mouth stank of Hennessey.

"I'm not dumb," growled Ben. Jadyn's two goons, Andy and Matt, shadowed behind him. Both their faces looked pale.

"Nah, you ain't. You just frickin' stupid," said Jadyn. He pushed Ben. If it had been anyone else Ben wouldn't have fallen.

Caught unawares at the suddenness of it all, Ben floundered on the icy sidewalk and landed on his ass in a puddle. The wetness soaked into his brand-new jeans.

Jadyn doubled over laughing. Andy and Matt glanced at one another, worry on their faces.

Ben's world changed color in front of his eyes. Red tinged his vision. His hands turned into fists.

Mia ran to help Ben get back to his feet, but Jadyn grabbed at her. She screamed as he lifted her, feet kicking ineffectually at the air. Jadyn stood at six-foot-eight and while he still had puppy fat, his strength in the last two years of high school had grown enormously.

"Let me go!" said Mia.

"Never knew you could turn into a hot-looking tasty slut," said Jadyn. His hand smacked Mia's bottom. The other hand groped at her small breasts.

Mia's face froze in shock and terror. Her brown eyes widened and she went limp as a statue, as if somebody sucked the life out of her.

Ben's anger erupted like a volcano. The anger that dwelled in him since the day Imperator Kaali murdered his father surged through his veins.

Ben pushed himself from the ground. He ran at Jadyn and jumped so he could reach his face. His fist slammed into Jadyn's face and the big kid stumbled back.

Mia fell to the ground.

Jadyn held up his hands, but Ben was already following in with another hit— this time right in the ribs. A left and right.

Jadyn bellowed and tackled Ben with double hands. They went crashing to the wet ground. The world twisted around Ben in a blur of Jadyn's smelly hoodie, sharp lights, and the red rage that covered his vision.

Eventually, hands pulled Jadyn and Ben apart and threw them to the ground.

A thin gray police robot held out its hands. Red and green lights blinked on the robot's shoulders. "Cease and desist or face immobilization."

Jadyn bounced back up and ran at Ben.

Ben ducked under the police robot's lanky legs and elbowed Jadyn right in the groin, and then as the bigger boy fell Ben jumped over him and slammed Jadyn in the face. One two. One two.

A screaming filled Ben's ears. Something yanked him hard. He caught the faintest flicker of the police robot holding out its hand and something blue like electricity crackling in the air. When the robot touched Ben the world exploded.

Ben fell to the ground. The red of his world changed to orange.

A crowd of kids from the arcade gathered around. Julie crossed her arms and trembled. Keith wrapped his hands around her and swallowed as he noticed the blood dripping from Ben. Nobody said a word. Mia kept crying.

Ben got to his knees and struggled toward Jadyn. He grasped Jadyn's ankles and the older boy whimpered. He looked down at Ben through split lips, a blackened eye, and blood-soaked face.

"Don't ever touch Mia," Ben said, raising his hand. The rage still boiled in him.

Behind Ben the police robot reached out a skinny gray hand and tasered Ben for the third time.

It was the first time that police robot had to taser a human three times in order to immobilize it.

Mia cried.

Chapter 10

Old Drunk

EDF Orientation Day
New York, Chinatown
31 November 2076
09:00

Ben grasped the bars of his cell and stared out forlornly at the walkway that lined the other cells in the local jail. All the cells lined out two meters by two meters, and Ben shared his with another drunk. The other guy reeked of alcohol and wouldn't shut up.

"You're a berserker, boy. I know I was one myself. That damn EDF, they just kick you out when they've used you. Be careful of them, boy," said the drunk.

Ben ignored him.

Jadyn lay in the adjacent cell, groaning as a nurse robot tended to his wounds. The big kid was lying on a bed with half his face wrapped in bandage. The nurse robot took his hands and sprayed something on them that healed the deep gouges there.

"You need to rest for twenty-four hours," the nurse robot said to him. "Please drink this." She held out a cup.

Jadyn struggled to sit up against the wall but the nurse robot helped him. He sighed as the nurse robot held the cup for him to sip.

Jadyn sipped at it and gagged. "What is it?"

"It is ultra-antibiotics. You have swelling of the liver, damage to your kidneys. You also have lots of bruises along your body, implying sustained damage. When did you get these bruises?" The nurse-bot had a single eye that whirred and clicked as it stared at Jadyn.

"Is this being recorded?" Jadyn asked. He looked nervous.

"Everything is always recorded," said the nurse-bot.

"I'm fine. Thanks," said Jadyn.

The nurse robot stood up and rolled out on its four wheels.

Ben wondered about the nurse robot's diagnosis. He didn't hit Jadyn that badly. He couldn't have. Jadyn must have sustained the other hits elsewhere. From someone else. But who?

"Rope yourself, Ben," Jadyn croaked.

Ben slammed his fist against the bars. "You want to go again? This time I'll kill you and leave you for dead." The words came out of his mouth without him even really thinking about it.

"Hey, calm down, berserker. You gotta learn how to control that," said the drunk behind him.

Jadyn gulped the drink the nurse-bot gave him and slumped back down to the bed. He looked defeated and tired.

"Get your hands off me," Ben said, turning around to face the drunk, annoyed.

The old drunk stared at Ben from a grizzly face. "Or what? You gonna beat up an old drunk like you did that helpless kid?"

"He wasn't helpless. He's a damn bully. Biggest ass bully in school. Look at the big overgrown fat turd now!" Ben shouted into the next cell.

"Hey, calm down, man," said the old man. "You're just a naive damn brat."

Ben beat against the bars. "Hello, officer? When do I get out of here?"

Footsteps sounded around the corner. A slim Latina woman with gray hair edging her temples put her hands against her hips.

"Tomorrow morning. When your parents come and get you. For now you shut up and lay low," said the police officer. She was in charge of the small jail that had five cells. Her desk was just around the corner.

"They aren't my parents. It's my guardian." Ben slumped to the ground and put his hands against his forehead.

100

A sonorous sound filled the air as Jadyn snored in the next cell.

"I wish I had a cup of whatever the nurse-bot gave him," Ben said to himself.

"That makes two of us, boy," said the drunk. "So how long you been a berserker for?"

"What are you talking about?" Ben said, annoyed.

The old drunk had an Asian look about him. He wore a singlet with an EDF tattoo on his left bicep. Six double fang marks surrounded the tattoo.

"Killed six Nagas while I was at the EDF," said the drunk, noticing that Ben was staring at his tattoos.

Ben scoffed. It was impossible to survive even killing one.

"Did you really?" he asked sarcastically. The old man nodded.

After the old man told him how he'd killed six Nagas, Ben realized he wasn't lying. Ben opened up and said, "I've messed up on the exams, got myself a low grade, and now I've been conscripted into the infantry. Yesterday I messed up Graduation. Last night was Family Day and I messed that up too. Ended up in jail." Ben knuckled his forehead. "I just wish—"

"—everything was like it was before Invasion Day?" finished the old man. He chortled softly as Ben looked at him with surprise. "I've thought that same thing over and over again. And you ain't the only one who messed up on Family Day."

"How long did you serve? What was it like? At the beginning?"

The old man had the shakes. His hands trembled as he clasped them across himself. Even though he looked frail and old there was something behind those bright green eyes.

"I don't like talking about it. The things we did and saw. It destroys them just as much as it does us." He paused and took a deep breath. "Boy, he ain't the enemy." The old man nodded to a bandaged and snoring Jadyn. "The Nagas are the enemy. He's just a pitiful kid with a drunk old man. I should know. I served with Amare Washington."

The old man's words hit Ben like cold water. Was that Jadyn's dad?

Ben said, "He grabbed Mia. I promised to keep Mia safe since we were little. And then when I saw that I just flipped. I couldn't control anything. The world turned red."

Ben shoved his knees up to his chest. The old man put his gnarly hands on Ben's knees.

"Boy, you've got it just like me. You gotta learn how to control that rage. Otherwise you gonna go crazy. Especially in the EDF. They will use you for it, boy. Squeeze all the rage out of you until…" He let his hands go and sat opposite Ben. "It ain't you that you have to look out for. It's the lives of your squad. People will be depending on you, man. You can't just flip out."

An awkward silence set in the cell, punctuated by Jadyn's snoring. After five minutes, Ben couldn't hold it in any longer. The old man kept staring at him with those wide spaced green eyes.

"What did you mean by berserker?"

"It's a type of fighter that uses a crazy rage to power them," said the old man. "The rage feels like it comes from here." He tapped his chest. "But it starts here really." He tapped his head. His gray hair fell in wisps around his ears, leaving the middle of his scalp hairless.

"I'm not an angry person," said Ben. He closed his eyes as a sharp pain rocked his temples. "I don't know what's happening to me. Recently it just feels like my head is about to explode." He had never ever told anybody how he felt. Not Julie, not his guardian. Not Mia.

They talked through the night until the early morning.

The old man's stories fascinated Ben. When the police officer said Ben only had an hour left before his guardian would come collect him, Ben asked the old man the question he wanted to ask most.

"What did you mean when you said the EDF love berserkers?"

"It's got to do with stimulant injections. This stimulant reacts well to berserkers and creates a super soldier at the expense of the berserker's health. They die fairly quickly as their adrenal glands and brain just turn to goop." He gripped Ben's arm. "Don't touch those injections. It cost me the lives of my entire squad.

The only reason I got an honorable discharge is 'cause I helped Onna."

A cold simmering fear curdled in Ben's gut. "But how do I get rid of it?"

"You can't get rid of it," said the old man, pressing his hands against his head. His voice made a keening sound as he cried.

A clanging sound came from beyond as the police officer opened the other cells. The families had come to collect their jailed loved ones. It looked to be all kids who had gone amok. Ben wondered if it was like this every Family Day.

"Ben!" Mia appeared through the passageway and ran to his cell. She stretched her hands through the bars and he clasped them. Her hands warmed him. He kissed her fingers through the bars.

"There, there, get back now," said the police officer, gently pushing Mia back. The officer swiped her hand across the cell's lock and the gate trundled open.

"Ben Williams, your family is here to release you," the police officer told him. She looked at the old man. "Jimmy Bugei-sha, your grand-niece is here for you."

A small Asian girl with fine features stalked into the cell and squatted to her feet and then hugged the old man.

"Zhi," said the old man. "It's time."

The young girl smiled forlornly at the old man and nodded.

Later Ben would realize he'd shared his cell with General Katana's uncle and curse himself. But right then he could only stare at the huge guy who stumbled after the officer cursing in a loud voice. This jail was getting quite busy again really quickly.

The officer went to the next cell. "Jadyn Washington, your father is here for your release."

A tall fat black guy came stumbling behind the officer. He looked like a much older and fatter version of Jadyn. He was mostly bald except for some gray dread-locks that hung over his forehead. His mud-stained shirt stank of alcohol.

He stumbled into the cell shouting. "You frickin' bum, did you sell them drugs like I tole ya? Where's the money?!"

Jadyn's eyes popped wide up and he pressed himself against the cell walls.

His father kicked him and before the police officer could stop him, he punched Jadyn on the side of the head, cracking his lips all over again.

"Mister Washington, you will restrain yourself," said the police officer. She shoved him against the side of the cell. "Make amends, Amare. Today is the first day of EDF orientation and most likely the last day you'll get to see your son."

"You should have died instead of Denzel. Where's the money?" Mister Washington said, even with the force of the officer pushing him against the wall. "I need that money. Got no liquid honey no more."

"I couldn't get none," said Jadyn, his voice quavering.

Ben couldn't believe Jadyn was lying on the ground like that. Jadyn flinched each time his father screamed foul words at him.

"Let me go!" Mister Washington shouted at the police offer. She slowly released her neck hold and told him to back away from his son.

"Frick you then," said Mister Washington. "Don't bother coming home." He threw Jadyn's EDF uniform on the floor. "Good riddance to you. You somebody else's problem now."

The police officer stood between Jadyn and his father. Mister Amare Washington strode out of the cell and just as he got out, he turned and hawked a goober. It flew into the air and smacked Jadyn on the face.

Ben caught Jadyn's eye right then and what he saw wasn't the huge bully Jadyn was school. What he saw was a scared kid building up a concrete shield around his fragile self to protect him against the outside world.

The police officer took a kerchief from her pocket and wiped the spit from Jadyn's face. "Your brother's death has got nothing to do with you. That's on the Earth Defense Force." She nodded to the entrance of the cell. "Let me take you to breakfast and then I'll drop you at the spaceport."

"C'mon, Mom's in the car," said Mia, looking at Jadyn with a sadness in her eyes. She tugged on Ben's arm. They walked through the passageway past the now empty cells.

"Did you know Jadyn's dad was a drunk?" Ben asked.

Mia's face fell. "Jadyn's brother died shortly after joining the EDF. Mom told me there were suspicious circumstances around his death. His dad is a vet from the times of Operation Black Mamba. Jadyn can't be blamed for how he is. It's this war. It's screwed up so many families."

"But yesterday. Did he hurt you?" Ben asked. So many confusing feelings warred inside of him.

"I'm okay. I was just more shocked than anything."

"Is your mom mad?" Ben asked.

"What do you think?" Mia asked.

Ben walked out into the cold New York air. Frost laid a sheen of patina across all the cars.

They got into the car and Annie, Mia's mom and Ben's guardian, stared at him briefly in the rear-view mirror.

"I'm sorry, Annie."

She turned around and faced him. "It's your father's death anniversary today. Do you want to go to the park?"

"No," he said. Somehow feeling that was the right answer. Something the old man in the jail had said sparked inside of him. "Just thanks for collecting me."

Chapter 11

Goodbye

Pyggy, Mia's pet snake, hissed at her in annoyance and slithered up her hand. *Me come with you*, he spoke in her mind.

Pyggy's mid-section was about the width of two markers but his head tapered into a pencil like silhouette. His russet brown patterning held a tinge of red dust. His species, the Pygmy Python, endemic to his far flung home of Australia. That's how Mia got the idea for his name.

"I'm going to outer space. You would stand out like a sore thumb," Mia said to him. "Mom will look after you, now."

Me sad, Pyggy said. Mia heard his distinct accent in her mind.

The first time she heard snakes speak was the year after Ben's dad had been killed. She'd been walking past Snakes'R'Us in the Lower East Side when she heard their screams. She didn't even pause but dashed into the pet shop where her ears were greeted by their screams and cries as they were murdered. A lot of snakes were culled after the Naga invasion. The once lucrative pet reptile trade stopped overnight. It was so stupid as snakes on Earth had nothing to do with giant sized snake aliens. But the Covid-19 pandemic had nothing to do with toilet rolls and still humans emptied the shelves of their local stores.

Mia burst into that shop and immediately spotted the uniquely looking pygmy python who was screaming at her because he didn't want to die. The pet store owner raised a butcher's cleaver over the python and was about to bring it down when Mia intervened.

She shook her head at the horrible memory.

"Don't be sad," said Mia. "I'll meet you again, when I come back."

Pyggy curled around her forearm. She caressed his beautiful scales and gently kissed him on the snout. *I come with you*, he said.

"You can't, they do complete x-ray, gamma ray, full strip searches before anyone gets admitted into the shuttle. That's not even in near the space station. When you get to the ISS-SDF you have to go through another bunch of checks before they allow you in." She scratched his belly. He loved that.

Hmrfh, nice, said Pyggy. He proceeded to doze like a necklace hanging around her neck.

Mia turned around to check to make sure she'd tidied everything. Apparently the SDF wasn't as strict as the EDF when it came to bringing personal possessions.

Mia made a final circuit around her room. Pictures of snakes of every shape, color, and species stared at her from her walls.

What surprised her was how much Ben loved snakes too. She thought he wouldn't hold them in good light because a giant snake killed his dad. But he was more curious about the Nagas than anything else. He was constantly filled with questions, even more than Mia. She learned how to be curious from him. Always asking questions, she thought, just like a kid. And then she felt sad as they would part company for the first time in their lives soon.

Mia stripped the bed sheets, the blanket and pillow covers, and put them into the laundry basket. Mom would use their empty rooms as guest rooms for visitors. She hoped people visited because she knew her mom couldn't take it being alone.

For a moment Mia paused there as she recollected the nightmare that plagued her last night. Slithery visions kept intruded in her mind. The smell of slithery things. The hiss of forked tongues. A Naga chasing her. Only when she turned to confront it - it was only a mirror image of herself.

"Time to go," Mia said to herself.

Hmmm, Pyggy murmured in his sleep.

Ben's bedroom held eight years of memories. His EDF recruit uniform lay at the foot of his bed with his nametag already on it. A baseball cap lay atop the clothes.

Apart from that everything else in the room reminded him of his childhood. A baseball bat hung from a cabinet next to his Naga-jitsu trophies. His father had gifted the bat to him on Ben's eighth birthday. It had his father's signature on the front: Oliver Williams.

An animated photo hung against the wall by the left side of the door. Taken only two years ago at Disneyland: Ben, Mia, and Annie. Annie stood in the middle with both her hands draped about her young charges. He stared at Annie's features. Mia's mom looked like an older and more elegant version of Mia. Annie had Mia's chocolate coloring but ripened with age. Unlike Mia, Annie had naturally blue eyes and stared into the picture with a sardonic smile. She must have been gorgeous when she was younger.

In the ten years Annie had looked after Ben, he'd never called her 'Mom,' she never asked him, and he'd never felt that way about their relationship.

She'd always been Annie to him.

Annie who'd taken him under her guardianship after that fateful day ten years ago.

Ben showered, shaved, and then put on his Earth Defense Force uniform. Recruits couldn't take a single thing to the base.

He stood at the foot of his bed looking around the room. He took the tablet by his study desk and wrote a letter to Annie. He set it to be emailed to her in twenty-four hours' time. He would be inside the base by then and cut-off from external communications.

He let out a long-held breath, turned, and left his room. Was Julie doing the same thing that very moment? His hands trailed over the banister as he walked down the stairs. For once he really looked at the pictures that lined the wall. So many of them showed him and Mia. The last one at the bottom of the stairs showed Mia, Ben, his father, Oliver, and Annie. The picture taken on that fateful day at the park.

He rested his forehead against the picture.

The stairs thudded behind him as Mia came running past. "Your last breakfast at home!"

Ben turned and followed her down into the kitchen. She wore a purple Space Defense Force uniform with a completely different patch on her left breast pocket: a purple planet with two yellow discs forming an X over it.

"That is a cool uniform," Ben said as they sat down. His green Earth Defense Uniform with the military patch didn't have the same flash.

"Morning, my darlings," said Annie as she bustled about in the kitchen. "I have made you both a hale and hearty breakfast. Scrambled tofu with caramelized onions and a side of wild mushrooms and smoked soy-bacon."

"Woo-hoo!" shouted Mia. "I'll make the chai." Mia loved making a super strong tea with ginger, cinnamon, cardamom, and cloves.

As Mia made the chai, Ben went to Annie. He smiled sheepishly. "Need any help?"

"Chop the mushrooms, darling."

He had meant to apologize about ending up in jail on Family Day but the words stuck in his tongue. That's why he'd written the letter. He wasn't good at saying things. So he just chopped the mushrooms.

After, as they sat on the dinner table, Ben had never eaten anything so delicious. He also hadn't eaten anything since last night at the arcade. The mushrooms burst with flavor in his mouth and the tofu had just the right spice and was a perfect match with the crunchy Panini bread and the drenched caramelized onions.

The house alarm chimed when it hit nine o'clock.

"All the kids will be dropped at the local tram station," said Annie.

Mia said, "Well, we're lucky the tram stop is just outside this house, right? The spacecraft comes and picks us up at eleven-thirty from New York Central Spaceport. We still have time."

They finished their food in contemplative silence. Today could be the last day Annie ever had with her two young charges.

"Hold hands," said Annie. Mia held out her hands and Ben clasped her hand to his right and Annie's to his left. They formed a ring. "Dear God, please bring my loved ones back safely and thank you for all the blessings you have showered us with."

Annie's face looked strained as she looked up. "Time to go, kids."

The tram stop stood just a five-minute walk away from their apartment. A huge multi-segmented tram that resembled a giant silver centipede hovered toward the local stop. The platform was crowded with kids all heading for the Earth Defense Force.

Mia hugged her mother tightly. She kissed her. Annie showered Mia's head with kisses. They both cried. Mia stepped back and Ben gave Annie a hug.

"Don't worry, Annie, nothing bad will happen to Mia. I'll bring her back," he said.

"Bring yourself back, too," Annie said.

But all Ben could see were those dozens of Earth Defense Force soldiers who got out of the tram as it stopped. They whistled for attention and began to shout out instructions to the kids.

Chapter 12

Bagged and Tagged

EDF Orientation Day
Australia, Nullarbor Region
31 November 2076
17:00

The Earth Defense Force Capital Base Oceania, known to the soldiers as EDF Australia HQ, stretched out across the entire horizon, occupying 600,000 acres. It divided itself equally into three sections: Army-occupied east, Air Force-occupied central, and Navy-occupied west.

A huge eight-lane runway stretched out in the middle of the Air Force section. Massive hangars surrounded the runway. Circular terminals stretched out from the hangars, and jet-gates stretched out from the terminals. Robotic vehicles zoomed across the runway carting fuel, ammunition, and people.

Inside the C-10M Super Titan, the five g-forces shoved Ben so hard that his vision grayed out. His backbone pressed against the hard seat. Just as he thought he couldn't handle it anymore the pressure decreased and the grayness disappeared, revealing the dome-roofed hangars edging the wide runway of the Earth Defense Force capital base through the oval windows.

"Argh," Ben called out. The slots in the floor tightened around his army boots, squishing his toes. Two holes in the ceiling sucked the straps around his shoulders to tighten them as the C-10M rapidly descended. The floor rumbled.

Five thousand kids stood just like Ben did, spread out through the five levels of the military's largest troop transport. He wondered if they were suffering as much as him. His answer came quickly enough.

The girl standing next to Ben vomited. The vomit hung in the air and then moved like a wet pancake to hit her right back in the face.

The girls and boys were from all over the world: Chinese, American, Malaysian, British, Thai, and others Ben couldn't make out where they were from. Most of the kids looked tired, a few hadn't stopped crying, and some just looked scared.

The C-10M picked up Ben's entire high school from the John F. Kennedy spaceport at 1300 hours. It was the carrier's third stop before it headed south. Flight time was only one hour to reach Australia from New York. There were lots of stops, though, which lengthened the journey. Eventually, the C-10M's shadow flew over the Southern Ocean as it descended toward the capital base.

With a resounding thump the C-10M landed on the EDF's tarmac. Outside, five huge towers rolled toward each side of the pentagon-shaped C-10M. Each of the towers consisted of five levels with extended ramps. The ramps connected to a different level in the aircraft.

"Get me out of this thing," said Jadyn from Ben's right side.

To economize space to fit five thousand troops, the C-10M had stripped itself of seats. Instead straps from the ceiling and lock points on the ground held the troops in place. They were packed together tighter than sardines.

Ben sighed in relief as the shoulder straps wound back into the ceiling slots and the floor slots loosened simultaneously.

"Oomph," said Jadyn, not anticipating the movement. "What the heck?" He stumbled to his knees, head-butting another kid in the back.

Or he would have accidentally hit the kid, who turned out to be a girl, but she somehow detected the movement at her back, slipped out of the safety straps, twisted and caught Jadyn. She put him on the ground and shoved her knees against his ribs with one fist held high.

Ben quickly stepped in between the girl and Jadyn. Even though she looked small there was something about the way she carried herself that gave Ben's brain a 'danger' alert.

"Hey, he didn't mean it, he's just heavy," Ben said, nodding at the safety straps.

The young girl's nametag said 'Zhi' and the small lettering below that said 'Bugeisha.' The standard meant everyone had their first names stitched in much bigger letters above their last names. A 3D barcode striped itself above the names.

A robotic voice announced through the speakers and echoed throughout the C-10M's cabin, "Attention recruits. You are now on Earth Defense Force Capital Base Oceania, Air Force section. Ensure the prompt relocation to your Army section."

Zhi smoothly stepped back, grabbed Jadyn's hand, and pulled him up effortlessly.

Ben's mouth dropped. The girl couldn't have been four-foot-nine. Jadyn stood at six-eight and weighed over one hundred twenty kilos. Zhi couldn't have weighed much more than a nine year old.

Zhi bowed at Jadyn. She blinked languidly, like a lizard sunning, and moved away in the same easy motion, as if she didn't effortlessly lift a boy who weighed a thousand times heavier than her.

"I didn't need your help, jerk," Jadyn said, pushing past Ben and heading to the exit.

Ben stared at the back of Zhi's shaved head. Who was she? His eyes widened as he recollected the memory. She was the girl who came to get that drunk old man he'd shared a cell with on Family Day.

The C10-M's floors shook as five thousand kids—a thousand on each level—marched out to the jet-gates that connected to the mobile towers.

Ben couldn't believe it as he walked across the jet-gate to the mobile disembarkation tower. He caught a glimpse of Capital Base Oceania spread all around.

The noise of five thousand kids talking mingled with the sounds of other C-10M spacecraft taking off. Huge mechs walked in the distance, clanging past hangars stocked with the meanest looking F33-Boomerangs. Drones carrying munitions made a pretty row of lights as they descended.

126

Ben lost his count at ten C-10Ms as he stepped into the disembarkation tower. As he entered the tower, he followed glowing signs to the upper level and pressed himself against the sides to watch. The towers rumbled and began to move away from the C-10M.

Four other towers filled with new recruits stood equidistantly around the C-10M, trundling away. Two huge aviation tankers with tires the size of an entire house made their way across the tarmac. The tires supported a bulging yellow belly filled with fuel. Umbilical cords snaked out from the top of the bellies and flew to plug themselves into the underbelly of the C-10M.

"I wonder where those G15-Venator's are going," said Andy, coming up behind Ben and moving to his right. A group of the quadcopters flew over the horizon.

"They don't waste time here," said Matt, who stood to Ben's left.

Jadyn's two goons respected him now after Ben beat the crap out of their leader. Ben still didn't really like them.

"Looks like they're prepping for war. Like right now." said Andy.

"Everything is huge. I mean I feel like a small bug. Check out those F33-Boomerangs!" said Matt.

Ben nodded. As soon as they disembarked, he'd felt the hugeness of the place press against him.

A group of F33-Boomerangs hovered out from their hangers. Their engines whined shrilly, and even as far as the boys were, over four kilometers away, the sound rang in their ears.

The F33's angular, jagged nose flared around a double canopy, the wings jutting out from a wide body dripping with missiles. Two angular fins sat over the twin turbines that began to glow with heat. They were the pride and joy of the Air Force, the most reliable jet fighters ever made.

A booming sound filled the air as ten of the F33s' thrusters fired from below their bellies and their vertical takeoff sent them hurtling into the air, where they quickly disappeared across the gray horizon.

"Well, here we are, first day of orientation. I wonder what they have in store for us," said Matt.

"Hey, look, there's the idiot, Natalie," said Andy, pointing to another corner of the tower. She sat huddled alone on a seat, staring at the floor.

"If you call her an idiot again, I'll smash your face," Ben said, pushing himself close to Andy. "Got it?" The Asian kid nodded and Ben pushed past him.

"Hey Natalie, check out this view," Ben said as he approached her.

She looked up at him. Her eyebrows curved up in surprise and then her lips crinkled into a smile.

"Really?"

He beckoned. "C'mon."

Ben, Natalie, Andy, and Matt kept staring out as the huge tower trundled toward the terminal gates. Their eyes reflected the activity around the base as it prepared for war.

The towers came to a stop. Ben and his friends followed the directions on the speaker and the glowing arrows on the side of the walls and on the grounds. Everyone kept in order. There wasn't any rushing.

Ben walked outside where he assembled into a large square. A man stood on a small crate. Two other soldiers stood by his side holding M18s.

"I hope you midgets like pain. I'm Sergeant Clinton. The first thing that will happen to you is your bagging and tagging. An incision will be made at the base of your neck and the EDF dog tag—a microchip—will be inserted. It'll hurt like hell. Now get inside for processing."

A huge hangar that looked like it was a barn house from a horror movie stared right at Ben.

They were told to march right inside.

🐍

The conveyor belt looked like it went straight to hell. Kids disappeared behind a big yawning black hole in the hangar wall marred with bullet holes and burn marks. They screamed as the hole in the

130

wall swallowed them. A flaring red light followed their screams.

"This is like a rollercoaster designed by the God of Hell," said Andy, who stood in front of Ben.

Ben just swallowed. Only moments ago he'd been joking with his friends about their new adventure and now the reality of the Earth Defense Force settled in.

Hangar 07 stretched out far and wide, over ten football fields long and five wide, with each segment broken up into sections. The kids formed a line at the very back, Hangar 07 Section A, around them a slew of artillery, drilling machinery, and the odd tank. Like a giant crazed snake slumped over its dead enemies, a conveyor belt ran through all of the equipment.

All the kids formed a line on either side of the conveyor belt. Two chairs sat on each slat of the belt. A never-ending row of chairs that streamed past so quickly it made the chairs blur.

The sergeant stood above and pulled on a lever and the conveyor came to a screeching halt.

"Row by row, get on and strap in," shouted the sergeant.

Matt and Andy stood in the row in front of Ben. They both clambered onto the conveyor and sat on the seats.

The seats looked old with wooden backs and worn leather pads in the back and butt areas. Nail heads revealed themselves through the joints. *Whenever these things were made was a long time in the past*, Ben thought.

He waited apprehensively for his turn, while about five hundred kids strapped themselves to the chairs. Andy looked at Ben and there was a fear and worry in his eyes.

A leather strap crossed Andy's wrist on either side and strapped his hands tightly against the wooden chair handle. The same happened on his leg near his knees and just at his ankles.

"It's tight as a fishes ass," said Andy, between gritted teeth.

Matt, who stepped in from the other side, looked pale. Sweat dotted his forehead. He kept holding his hand to his mouth like he was going to puke.

"Ooh-rah, ready as she goes," the sergeant shouted, and then he pulled down on a lever.

A clanging sound reverberated around the hangar. The entire conveyor belt now filled with kids on the two-by-two seats shot forward. It twisted as it went around.

"Good luck!" Ben shouted as Andy and Matt shot forward. The rattling the conveyor belt made had Ben covering his ears.

"Next," said Sergeant Clinton. He wore a savage grin across his face. Somehow, he seemed immune from the heat in the hangar and didn't sweat.

Ben swallowed as he took his seat. Beside him Natalie smiled. Was she looking forward to this? She got in and snapped the buckle over her hips. It made an audible click. "C'mon, let's get this over and done with."

Ben stared at her. She was eager.

All this time a group of corporals was yelling at them to quickly get onto the conveyors.

"Hurry up and get your butt on there, soldiers! We've got to tag and bag a hundred thousand of you. There are many more recruits incoming."

Ben's heart beat rapidly. A sour taste filled his mouth. The entire conveyor belt filled itself with kids and then the next thing he heard was a clunk.

The conveyor belt shot forward, faster than a rollercoaster. Natalie screamed. Ben screamed. Before he knew it, he was taken through the wall.

Up ahead giant-sized robots with spider-like hands twirled and stopped. Their sharp hands zapped against the kids. There was a flaring of color and noise and then the kids ahead of them slumped in their chairs.

The conveyor belt screeched to a halt. Natalie's hand reached for his and Ben clasped it. They couldn't get out and the straps on their shoulders dug in deeper as they got closer to the robots. The straps shoved them in so their butts made impressions against the seats.

Ben's turn came.

A huge robot hand whipped toward him. He couldn't even move his neck. The robot's hand consisted of sharp blades that caught the dim light. Its black chassis made it look like an undertaker. Heat scalded Ben's scalp and he screamed in pain. His entire vision covered as the robot's hand cupped his forehead and held it in place.

Another sharp hand shoved itself against the back of his neck and injected something right into his skin. It burned and hurt so bad that Ben lost consciousness.

Could he be dead already? The last thought he had was that he wished he could see Mia one last time to give her a big hug and tell her how much he loved her.

And then he was gone.

Chapter 13

Operation King Cobra

Freedom Stadium hunched in the middle of Capital Base Oceania like a relic from the ancient past. Shavings of curled paint littered the ground along the walls, revealing the original gray concrete. Rust covered the huge east and west gates. A faded giant poster of the Sharks, the local military football team, stared down at a row of turnstiles long since decommissioned. The Earth Defense Force logo appeared below the Sharks' poster with a list of names that couldn't now even be read.

It was as if Freedom Stadium, the beating heart of the capital base, had given up. The wide passageways once pounded with the steps of thousands of soldiers and their families as they visited to watch the Earth Defense Force Super Bowl. Now dust, dead insects, and a few deflated gridiron balls were the only occupants.

But tonight life inhabited Freedom Stadium.

General Katana stood in the center of the football field on a raised platform addressing the one hundred thousand new recruits that stood at attention in front of the seats where screaming fans once sat. A Wild-Boar Jeep parked itself next to the platform, its rear gun turrets pointed up into the air. Dozens of elite Black Berets, armored to the teeth, formed a circle around the platform.

"This is humanity's darkest hour. If we do not succeed humanity will be wiped out from the face of the Earth," said General Katana. She took a deep breath. "Welcome, all one hundred thousand of you." She turned and saluted one of three spherical drones flying around her.

It had a long stalk with a bug-eyed lens that captured video. "2nd Foot Soldier Battalion, from Capital Base Afro-Eurasia, I salute you." She saluted the next drone. "4th Foot Soldier Battalion, from Capital Base Americas, I salute you." She saluted the last drone. "3rd Foot Soldier Battalion, from Capital Base Antarctica, I salute you."

"And finally, to my own base: 1st Foot Soldier Battalion, Capital Base Oceania. I salute you." She turned and saluted all one hundred thousand new recruits who stood in the stands of Freedom Stadium.

Even though Ben stood at the upper end of the stadium far away from General Katana, he felt her presence like warm heat. A sliver of sweat oozed down his forehead and tickled his nose. He desperately wanted to scratch it.

The General continued her talk. "Not long ago this capital base held the beating hearts of fifty-five million soldiers. Twenty million of those brave souls perished in Operation Black Mamba, ten years ago. Twenty-four million more brave soldiers paid the ultimate sacrifice only two months ago in Operation Python. Today a skeleton crew operates all four of our capital bases." Behind the General, still images appeared showing buildings hulking in the dark, black eyeless pits where brightly lit windows would've been. The runway empty of traffic. And miles and miles of unlit buildings.

Ben remembered marching to the barracks. On his way there he'd passed lots of empty buildings. Now he understood.

"There are four hundred thousand active combatants left. Everyone must be fully committed to Operation King Cobra. You, me, us." Her hands pointed to a soldier near her, then to herself, and finally she made a gesture that encompassed all one hundred soldiers in Freedom Stadium and the three hovering drones.

"Today I will talk to you about Operation King Cobra that will be launched in three months' time. And the role you are expected to play. We will succeed. We have learned from our failures in Operation Python." As she began to narrate the mission objectives of Operation King

Cobra, a huge display flared to life behind her showing the attack plan.

Ben couldn't believe it. Normally it took five years of training before new recruits were even allowed to join the most basic mission. Here he was, only eighteen, and sure he'd gone through seven years of a military curriculum at school, but now he was listening to mission parameters and expected to partake in them.

Ben's mouth dried. His heartbeat weakened. An ominous feeling stole over him. What were four hundred thousand soldiers against the Nagaplex when forty-four million died doing the same thing?

The General's voice tore Ben out of his dark thoughts. She said, "We are going to change history! We are attempting to do something that has never been done since Invasion Day: successfully infiltrate the Nagaplex, kill all the Naga hatchlings, and destroy the Nagaplex."

The huge display showed the soldier body-cam footage taken from the General herself during Operation Python three months ago.

The hatchling cavern spread as far as the eye could see. It was the inside of those long sharp horns, Ben realized.

"This will be a joint operation between all the divisions within the Earth Defense Force. The Air Force, the Navy, and the biggest effort will come from the Army."

Ben wondered if Julie and Mia would be involved. Could Julie learn to pilot an F33-Boomerang within three months? What was Mia doing up in the Space Defense Force? It seemed unlikely that he would see either of them ever again.

"Listen carefully, as you will need to go over this every single day until you memorize these sequences." The display above showed an animation sequence of several C-10M Super Titans depositing soldiers in the middle of the Australian desert.

"Remember the middle of the Australian desert is a contained radiation zone. The C-10M's will deploy all the EDF infantry soldiers on the ground. That is all the new recruits in this year's intake—four hundred thousand infantry."

The animation showed four arrows—east, west, north, south—each of the four battalions deployed at each arrow. Each section stood equidistantly from each other, forming a cordon around the Naga-plex in the middle.

"This section is called the graveyard," said the General, pointing at the perim-eter of the Nagaplex. As she pointed a red laser dot marked the area. "This is where millions of EDF soldiers died. It is a graveyard, not just for us, but for the Nagas too. We have killed many of the blue Nagas, the drone-hunters, which are their equivalent of infantry soldiers. Though not as many as we would like."

The red laser dot passed the graveyard and highlighted the Nagaplex itself.

"Once past the graveyard, we will enter the Nagaplex itself. This frontal assault will occupy the attention of the Nagas." General Katana stepped to the side as a black-clad official appeared and took her spot.

"I am Chief Admiral Evelyn Wilson, leader of the Space Defense Force."

Ben eyes widened. Was this Mia's leader? Ben would call Mia when he got the chance. He needed to know she was okay.

"Whichever squad makes it into the Nagaplex will escort a group of Space Defense Force scientists into the Naga-plex's hatchery. Once there you will obey their commands. Once the SDF person-nel have executed their task, you are to escort them back out of the Nagaplex to the designated LZ."

The map showed red dots pointing to a Landing Zone right at the middle of the graveyard.

"It is critical that the Space Defense Force personnel carry out their mission with success. Failure to do so may result in failure of the entire mission even if you kill all the hatchlings and destroy the Nagaplex."

What could be more important than those two things? Ben thought. *What is the Space Defense Force hiding? What aren't they telling us?* He got the cold chills and turned to see Natalie looking at him.

She shook her head and gave him a thumb's up. *Can't wait*, she mouthed.

Ben thought she was crazy. He couldn't help but feel this was very bad. Had any recruit cohort ever been tasked with going to war in such a short time?

Chapter 14

Close To The Edge

Overheard conversation between General Katana and Chief Admiral Evelyn Wilson.

"Put them on the neural-helmets. And quadruple the accelerant speed."

"No, I'm not doing that. It's too dangerous."

"Operation King Cobra executes in three months. I've got ninety days to turn children into seasoned veterans. Day one is over and you and I are still talking."

"That's why I wanted to talk with you face to face. The last time we tested NPR in Operation Python was on a gradual dosage over a one-year period. Side effects included—"

"I know what the side effects were. Firsthand. There is no time."

"But quadruple accelerant speed? It means they will suffer four times as—"

"—quickly and their brains could turn into mush. But they will be on a combo of NPR and NGH and we know the NGH can act as a counter."

"I'm also hypothesizing you want the NGH administered at the same rate?"

"Yes."

"God save us. The NGH will age them by ten years in three months. Onna, have you told them?"

"This is our last attempt, Evelyn. Humanity will go extinct if we fail."

Chapter 15

Alpha One Tango

The army barracks sprawled out before Ben in a vast array of ten by ten blocks. Each block rivaled the size of a football field. He marched toward the barracks exiting from the hangar bay area where orientation finished. The wide roads sloped down. He felt tiny against the backdrop of this gigantic base.

Ben remembered his dad telling him a Jack the Beanstalk story during the nights he couldn't sleep as a child. That was

how he felt now: like a little human tres-
passing in a giant's backyard. Ben didn't
belong here.

Jadyn marched behind him, and
Natalie marched behind Jadyn. The Japanese girl, Zhi, Ben met aboard the C10-M
Super Titan marched in front of him
too. She'd hardly said a word since their
disembarkation.

Sergeant Clinton led the entire group.
When they reached the barracks courtyard
they stopped. The courtyard stretched out
wide. Three flagpoles stood in the center.

"At ease," said Sergeant Clinton. "You
have been assigned your squads and your
squad leaders. You will now stow your
gear into your bunks. You have five minutes to hit the canteen for chow."

🐍

A hundred beds stretched out in the
room. Two bunks per row. When the one
hundred recruits stood to attention inside
the bunker, Sergeant MacAndrews began
to read out the squads.

Ben jumped when his name was called alongside several others.

"Squad Alpha One Tango, your Squad Leader is Zhi Bugeisha. Squad members are as follows: Ben Williams, Jadyn Washington, Natalie Sinclair."

Ben's eyes met the eyes of his school friends. The person in charge of their squad did not come from their school. A feeling of resentment flared through Ben. Why is that the case? he thought. Judging by the look on Jadyn's face he felt the same. Ben didn't envy Zhi the task of leading Jadyn. He would definitely challenge the diminutive Japanese girl.

"Attention!" shouted Zhi Bugeisha abruptly, swiveling toward them. She raised her hand in a salute.

Ben, caught unawares, gave a sloppy salute back, surprised at the loud voice that came from the small girl. Jadyn took his time and gave a desultory wave.

"Follow on three. One, two, three," Zhi Bugeisha did a spin and marched toward the end of the room.

Ben followed close behind her. Jadyn muttered beneath his breath, "A small little girl is our squad leader? We're going to be Naga meat."

Natalie gave a sidelong glare at Jadyn. Those two had never reconciled from their high school enmity. Or rather, Jadyn's constant bullying of Natalie still occurred even now.

Zhi gave no indication she'd heard Jadyn's comments.

"This is where we will sleep. There are no names to designate the bunks. Select a bunk and keep to it for the duration of our stay on base. Alongside your bunks is a receptacle recessed against the wall to store your M18s. At the base of your bed is a closet for you to store your clothes. Clothes will match the outline exactly that's illustrated inside the closet.

"Please get changed into your uniforms and be ready. We will head down to the mess hall as soon as you're done," Zhi said. "Do you have any questions?"

"Squad Leader, where do we get dressed?" asked Natalie.

"Right here," said Zhi.

All the other squads started changing right then and there. The girls and the boys in the same area.

Natalie's face reddened.

"We are soldiers, recruit. Get used to it," said Zhi.

Ben quickly went to his bunk and shoved his M18 into the side holster. The side holster swished back into the side of the bed. He quickly took off his clothes. He had never been in a room with so many women undressing before. It was hard not to take a peek.

Zhi's slender and slim body looked elegant. Her tightly corded muscles on her back and calves made her seem like an elite athlete. She turned and caught Ben looking.

"Okay, I'm outta here," said Jadyn. He'd already dressed in his new army uniform. His untucked shirt and unlaced boots made him look like a resident Manhattan artist.

"I didn't give you permission to leave," said Zhi. "And you haven't passed dress inspection. Not dressed like that." She stopped him in his tracks by stepping right in front of him.

Jadyn towered over her. Ben knew firsthand what that felt like. He remembered the first time he'd met the bully.

The two of them stared at each other. Zhi didn't move.

"Who the heck voted you our leader?" asked Jadyn.

"General Katana selected all squad leaders personally," said Zhi.

Jadyn's eyebrows rose in surprise. "Well, I didn't."

A few other recruits turned to look at the confrontation. Ben's stomach made a sinking sensation. He felt a touch on his arm and turned to see Natalie all dressed. Her uniform looked neat with the shirt tucked in, the pants tucked into the boots, and the boots laced. Even her stray red hair tucked itself neatly under the cap.

"Squad Leader," said Natalie. "We're ready."

Zhi's left eyebrow rose. She pointed to Natalie. "Like that."

Jadyn muttered underneath his breath and stomped to where Ben and Natalie formed a line. He quickly made himself presentable.

Zhi walked back toward them. The other kids' curious gazes turned away as they realized there would be no confrontation.

But Ben knew otherwise. Jadyn would confront Zhi physically. Eventually.

He just hoped it wouldn't be anytime soon.

𝓰

Dinner consisted of soya-skewers, long grain rice, and green vegetables with soy-beef. A side of dairy-free chocolate mousse sat on the left of the plate, along with a cup of hot peppermint tea. It tasted bland but it filled Ben right up.

Each table consisted of twenty seats, which meant five squads. Ben, Natalie, and Zhi sat at the edge of their table. Jadyn avoided them, going to the other end.

The only sounds in the mess hall consisted of the ding of the steel spoons against the steel plate. The occasional burp.

Ben licked his lips. Natalie just stared at her plate and ate her dinner quietly. Zhi ripped at her food like she'd been starved for a year. Ben considered himself a fast eater, yet Zhi finished her food in three minutes.

Hoping to break the awkwardness for his squad, Ben tried to make conversation. "Do you guys know that before severe global warming people would eat meat?"

Natalie's fork paused its journey. "No way."

Ben nodded. "Yes way. They even had this dish called steak."

She laughed. "Like a stake to the heart of Dracula?"

Ben frowned. "Well…" Was Natalie playing with him?

Zhi's wide eyes slanted downward. It gave her an air of poise. A slash of black eyebrows hovered over each eyes. A small scar crawled in the middle of her forehead. Her lips were a bright red, so unusual it made it seem like she wore makeup. But she gave Ben the impression she didn't think much about makeup.

Zhi said, "Each day we will burn five thousand calories. By the time we ship out for Operation King Cobra we will be too lean to be combat effective if we do not chow down a minimum of five thousand calories a day. Basically, that's twice what a normal person should eat. But that's a minimum for us. If we can't keep that up there isn't a use in us being here." She tapped her silver plate and it rattled against the table. "This here is one thousand five hundred cals."

"Lucky I have a bit of puppy fat," said Ben, trying to put some levity into the situation.

"Tomorrow you will wish you had eaten your five thousand cals." Zhi didn't bat an eye. She took her plate and elegantly stepped out of the wide bench, and headed back for a second serving.

"I don't think we got the most charismatic leader," said Ben.

Natalie, who had been halfway through putting a spoon of long grain rice into her mouth, sprayed it out all over her plate. She banged her hand against the table in a loud laugh. She mimicked Zhi's serious tone. "You will eat your five thousand calories."

It was such a perfect mimicry that Ben found himself laughing. Several of the other kids at the table turned to see what was so funny, but Ben just smiled back at them.

Only, Zhi didn't go for a second serving. She returned holding a rectangular tray with twenty purple vials sitting ensconced within foam.

Zhi said, "This is NGH. Every night after chow you are to self-administer your dosage. That is four vials per soldier per night." She held up a thin cylindrical vial. "Each dosage uniquely crafted for you." She grabbed two vials. As she touched one the vial beeped an alarm and a red light emitted from the top of it. "This means it's not for me. The doses are tracked against our chips." She patted behind at the nape of her neck, where their microchip dog tag had been installed that very day.

"The chips in our necks perform wireless authentication against the vials. And even if you manage to take the wrong dosage you will vomit it out. They all are clearly identifiable by the rows in this tray." She pushed the tray to the middle of the table. Each row held their full names and a vertical border around the four vials.

156

"Why would anyone want to take somebody else's dose?" Natalie asked.

"Today you will take your full four doses at once," said Zhi, ignoring her question. "Tomorrow we will go on the normal dosage cycle. The first as soon as you wake up at 0600, second at 1400 after lunch, third at 1700, and the fourth before bed at 2200."

"Wow, that's awesome," said Jadyn, reaching for his set of vials. "I'm gonna get big. Ooorah!"

"Are there any side effects?" Ben asked.

Zhi's eyes didn't flinch when they met his. *God*, Ben thought, *she has the eyes of an Undead Warrior.* Zhi grabbed a vial under her name and shoved it against the vein at the crook of her elbow. The vial's mouth popped audibly and hissed as the purple fluid drained into Zhi's vein.

"The side effect is that you may survive against the Nagas."

Dinner turned out uneventful. Asking Zhi about herself yielded nothing of significance. Natalie and Ben talked to one another and he was surprised to discover how funny she was. He felt an increasing guilt at being a part of the group who'd bullied her in high school. Being her friend here wasn't like at school where everyone would call Ben a loser; here nobody cared.

They headed back to the barracks, but Natalie pulled him aside and they hid under the shadows cast by a huge stack of munition crates.

"I think something bad happened in Zhi's childhood. She's got scars all over her body. And also, well, I can just tell. She hasn't answered a single question you asked about herself. Not even little stuff. We should investigate her last name."

Ben's curiosity got the better of him. "How?"

Natalie freckles glowed in the dark as she frowned. "What if she's some type of psycho? And she's our Squad Leader."

"I don't think the Earth Defense Force would do such a thing, right? I mean they're the good guys," said Ben.

"We don't have access to any database. Do you know anyone who does?" Natalie asked.

Ben clicked his fingers. His eyes widened. "Hey, Mia is in the Space Defense Force. She would have way higher clearance than us. I could ask her."

"Teamwork." Natalie raised her hand.

Ben high-fived her. She had a funny laugh punctuated with snorts.

They walked back into the barracks. And speaking of the devil.

"We get six hours to sleep but when we sleep, we have to wear this," said Zhi, standing at the end of her bed. She held out a thin helmet and turned it so they could see the inside. The interior consisted of a skullcap made out of gel that looked small and stringy, dangling down like veins. Zhi shoved the helmet over her shaved head and it made a sucking noise as if it were alive. "It's a neural helmet."

"What does it do?" asked Natalie.

"Accelerated learning. Basically stuff is downloaded into your head so you learn it like a real soldier on the battlefield. We deploy in three months. It's impossible with traditional training methods to prepare us adequately," Zhi said.

"Awesome! Why the heck they didn't have this in high school? Could've passed all those crap Mister Hackle subjects." Jadyn enthusiastically shoved his helmet on.

"What are the side effects?" Ben felt a foreboding steal over him. First those growth vials and now a neural helmet? He'd never heard anything about this back in school.

"Squad, let me be clear. Unless I state otherwise these instructions are mandatory. We aren't in the civvy world anymore. There are very few optional instructions in the EDF. Lights go out in five minutes. Put the helmets on, now."

Ben's helmet bore a digitized urban camouflage pattern on the outside shell. Vents at the top and sides of the helmet made it breathable. It was fairly light. Inside at the back he he found tiny lettering that said: NPR-v1. He wondered what that stood for? Maybe it was the revision number of the helmet? It meant they must have made a few versions.

Sighing, he shoved the helmet on. Thanks to their buzz cuts the helmets fitted on nicely. Within moments Ben lay on his bunk and looked up at Natalie's bed over his. Tonight would be his first night at the base.

Sleep beckoned as the helmet warmed his head. And he soon found himself thinking of home. Except that didn't happen. He suffered a nightmare and it felt so real. Like he fought the Nagas himself and died.

When he woke up six hours later it didn't feel like he'd slept at all. A small side receptacle in the wall ejected a tray that held a purple vial. Ben reached for it hesitantly. All around him all the other kids woke at the same time and reached for their doses.

Ben's hand clasped the vial. He shoved it to the vein on the crook of his elbow. A cold sensation shook him. It woke him up and increased his heart rate.

It made coffee seem like baby milk.

He felt great. He wondered why he'd been so paranoid about it before.

Chapter 16

Best Friends

Two weeks later...

Infantry Barracks
14 December 2076
24:00

Ben pressed his index finger against the scanner by the receptacle on his bed and the tablet computer swiveled out. He tilted it at an angle so he could look down, and rested his back against the bed stand. Scanning the military directory on the EDF's intranet, he couldn't find Mia's contact details.

"You're trying to call Mia, right?" Natalie's upside-down shaved head stared at him from above.

He frowned, feeling annoyed. "Yeah, but that's—"

"Wrong intranet. I sent her a message asking her about some stuff. Need to use the sdf.net not the edf.net I know, confusing huh?"

Ben was about to say, *That's none of your business*, but he perked up and said, "Well, thanks, Nat, appreciate it."

Natalie's head turned sideways. It was disconcerting staring at somebody who turned their head from an upside-down position. "That's the first time somebody has given me a nickname. I like it. Thanks." Her head disappeared.

"You're welcome, I guess…" Ben said. He changed the intranet to sdf.net/directory.com and searched for Mia. He found her right away. A photo of her in a purple Space Defense Force uniform. She totally rocked the picture in an adult way. Her title read: Special Projects Lead Scientist.

When Ben checked whom she reported to, his eyes bugged out. Mia reported directly to Chief Admiral Evelyn Wilson, the head of the Space Defense Force. How was that even possible?

"You should tell her," said the disembodied voice belonging to Natalie.

Ben looked up. "Tell her what?"

Natalie's upside-down face peered at him. "How you really feel."

"What are you talking about?" Ben asked, feeling irritated. "I grew up with Mia. Her mother is my legal guardian. She's practically my sister."

"Then you know she's not a psycho. You're practically already married in that case. It's a safe bet." Natalie cackled and her head disappeared.

Ben paused for a second, his finger hovering over Mia's picture. The epiphany that struck him was that Natalie was actually happy. She'd been completely miserable at school with all the bullying. And the stuff with her dad.

But Ben, all he wanted to do was rewind time to before the Nagas invaded. Since his dad died life had sucked.

Sighing, he pressed Mia's picture on the directory and the word 'calling' appeared over her picture. The calling sound went on for a few seconds too long and Ben was about to give up when Mia's face appeared. At first it was super fuzzy and then it cleared up somewhat. There was a huge lag.

"Benny!" Mia screamed in delight.

Ben smiled in embarrassment. He was in his barracks that he shared with a hundred other recruits. Everyone near him turned and stared. Matt and Andy got up from their beds and came closer. Ben turned the tablet to face the wall and sat his back against the wall away from the two goons. They were such doofuses, though they'd both grown on him since coming to base. They were actually super funny.

"How have you been?" he asked. "You're looking dapper in your directory profile. You're the big scientist now."

"I've been good. Here, look at my room." Mia took the tablet in her hand and spun around too quickly for Ben to notice much except that her room was huge.

"You've got a room all to yourself? Check this," he said, unplugging the tablet and pointing it in a semicircle. "This is where I stay."

Mia laughed. "It's probably because you need to bond with your team."

"Ben wants to bond with you, young hot thing!" Andy shouted, as he sat on Ben's bed and waved at her.

"Get away," said Ben, shoving Andy off his bed, only to realize Matt had come to the other side.

"Hello, Mia, I'm Matt. How long have you known Ben for?" Matt waved into the tablet and asked.

"Hello Matt," Mia said, her eyes widening. "Hey, you're the guitarist from The Radical Rascals!"

"Yeah, that's it." Matt grabbed Ben's tablet and swung it to Andy.

"I'm the lead singer!" said Andy, waving at Mia. "You remember us? Hey, when are you and Ben getting married?"

"Give it to me!" Ben shouted, but Jadyn laughed and shoved him back. It was the smile on his face that disarmed Ben. They'd been mortal enemies only two weeks ago.

"We've been best friends since childhood," said Mia.

Andy said, "I married my best friend."

"Really?"

"Give that back to me," said Ben, struggling past Jadyn.

And then to Ben's total horror all the kids around him began to chant, "Marry Mia," over and over again until it rang through the entire barracks.

It was the most embarrassing day in Ben's eighteen years of life. Eventually, he wrestled the tablet from Matt's hands and ran out of the barracks.

"Sorry about that," Ben said. "So you've seen a lot of people in my barracks. Do you work with anyone interesting?"

"Evelyn's kinda intense, if you call that interesting."

"You're on first name basis with the head of the Space Defense Force?"

Mia waved her hand. "It's not like that."

For a few more minutes they chatted and Ben couldn't help but feel there was an undercurrent of awkwardness throughout it all. Ben was about to say his goodbyes when Mia looked left and right as if she suspected somebody was listening in on her.

"Ben." Her voice dropped to an urgent whisper. Her face occupied the entire camera. Up close he could see the worry on her face and the dark bags underneath her eyes.

"Yeah, what is it?"

"Did they give you the NGH?"

His forehead furrowed. What was she talking about?

"It looks something like this." She held up a purple vial.

"Ahh yes, the growth hormone stuff. Yeah, today I had four already."

Mia looked left and right again. Her lower lip trembled. Her head shook from side to side. "Don't—" Her mouth moved but no sound came from the tablet. LINK DOWN blinked in red and the video call died.

Ben shook the tablet. "Mia?" He swiped. Nothing happened. He turned the power on and off. Nothing happened. He stared at the tablet. Had it just died? What was she going to say to him?

Chapter 17

What We Do For Love

From: Evelyn Wilson (evelyn.wilson@sdf.gov)
To: Mia Johnson (mia.johnson-patel@sdf.gov)
Subject: Project Einstein
[CLASSIFICATION: TOP SECRET]

Mia,

Sorry, your current permissions don't grant you access to the SIDE EFFECTS folders. I've granted you these permissions but it will take a few days. For now I've attached your request below:

Project Einstein (Neural Pathway Reconditioning)

Project Hulk (Neural Growth Hormone)

Let's book in a meeting. I want to know why you think this research can help you.

SIDE EFFECTS - Neural Pathway Reconditioning

***NPR-v01: ALL of the below (side effects include all of the below)

NPR-v02: Apotemnophilia (irrational desire to chop off your own limbs)

NPR-v03: Boanthropy (thinking you are a cow)

NPR-v04: Capgras Delusion (illusion of being surrounded by imposters)

NPR-v05: Clinical Lycanthropy (belief that you can morph into a werewolf)

NPR-v06: Cotard Delusion (belief that you are walking dead)

NPR-v07: Diogenes Syndrome (uncontrolled hoarding, self-neglect, apathy)

NPR-v08: Dissociative Identity Disorder (multiple personalities)

170

NPR-v09: Factitious Disorder (obsession with being sick)

NPR-v10: Kluver-Bucy Syndrome (memory loss, desire to have sex with inanimate objects)

***Currently administering this to our EDF infantry.

SIDE EFFECTS, MINOR - Naga Growth Hormone

Even though there are ten versions of the growth hormone (NGH-vA to NGH-vJ), these side effects are universal across the entire range:

Hypertension

Cataracts and Glaucoma

Easy bruising

Insomnia

Accelerated aging

Uncontrollable hand or limb movement

Rapid shrinking and expanding of joints

Tongue lesions

Explosive head syndrome (mind thinks explosions are happening everywhere)

Fish odor

We are currently administering NGH-vJ to our EDF infantry. While version J is the fastest and suits our current deadlines, it also has the worst accelerated aging.

ʔ

Space Station
14 December 2076
24:15

The knock on Mia's door came right after her call terminated with Ben. She jumped at the thudding sound and her tablet clattered to the ground.

She went closer to her door. Her entire body shook. She'd broken protocol and she had no doubt her call was blocked because of classified information. Data classification was the first thing they'd told her about two weeks ago when she'd been a brand-new recruit.

Mia didn't want Ben to take the learning accelerator or the growth hormone. He would suffer for the rest of his life. Not only that, but out of all the versions of these biological modifiers, the Earth Defense Force was using the strongest versions with the highest dosages and severest ramifications.

The Earth Defense Force would kill its own troops.

She remembered the history of war. Agent Orange used by the American government in the Vietnam war caused cancer and all sorts of other problems in their own soldiers, not to speak of the terrible cost it had on Vietnam's forests, and newborn infants.

The knock on the door came louder. The square display screen showed two black uniformed Space Defense Force soldiers.

Her hand shook as she pressed the door button. The door twirled open.

"Lead Scientist Johnson-Patel, you have been summoned by the Chief. Please step this way," the soldier said. His robotic voice came from behind a gray mask. An emblem of a drop pod etched against the armor on his left shoulder, indicating he belonged to the Planetfall Troopers, the infantry division of the Space Defense Force.

"Okay," Mia said, swallowing. She still wore her stained lab coat from the day's work.

Two more soldiers joined them as they exited Mia's room. Mia walked right in the center surrounded by four soldiers. She elicited many stares from the other Space Defense Force personnel as she strode toward the transport hub.

Within five minutes Mia stood in front of huge double oak doors with golden lettering: 'Chief Admiral Evelyn Wilson.' One of the soldiers pushed the door open.

"You may leave her with me," came the voice from behind the chair. The chair was turned away from Mia, so she could only see its back.

"Yes, sir," the soldier said with a crisp salute.

Mia was left alone in the Chief Admiral's room.

The chair turned around slowly, showing her the Chief, who was holding a tablet. The tablet displayed a recording of Mia's call with Ben only moments ago. Her heart felt like it would drop to the floor.

"I've followed you since you were five. Before Invasion Day. Back then I was an intelligence officer in the US Air Force. We had a top-secret program looking for kids that exhibited special talents. We found you. We didn't take you away from your family. We didn't tell the world what you had. We just monitored. And then Invasion Day happened and the Nagas put a bracelet on you, and on a lot of other gifted kids. That's the day we realized how powerful you really could be. The bracelet amplified your power. You're special, Mia." Evelyn left her table and walked to Mia. She crossed her arms. "But even special people are not allowed to break the rules."

Mia froze. It took several moments before she could move again. Nobody knew about her special talents. Nobody. Not even her mother. Instead she found herself saying, "I couldn't let him take those things. The growth hormone and the learning accelerant are evil. They're going to be the death of Ben."

"Do you think we made those decisions without thought to their ramifications? This is going to be our last attack, Mia. A last desperate lunge of the blade. The strongest versions of the growth hormone and the learning accelerant happen to have the worst side effects. That's not why we chose them. We have four hundred thousand children to train into soldiers in three months. For one last desperate attack. That's it. Do you understand?" Evelyn's hands pushed against Mia's shoulders. "Humanity will become extinct if we fail."

"They're my friends," Mia said.

"Ben's greatest threat will happen during Operation King Cobra in two and a half months' time. The survivability of an infantry soldier dropped into a Naga-infested LZ is sixty seconds. That is without the growth hormones and learning accelerant. With them, his chances of survival are at thirty minutes. Enough for us to get a squad into the Nagaplex."

The Chief strode back to her desk and grabbed a worn-out folder. It was marked with the words TOP SECRET in red. The side tab read 'Project Sunflare.' She handed Mia the folder.

"You love him, don't you?" the Chief said. "I loved a woman once and I lost her to the Nagas. I wish I had the power to change that." A long elegant finger with a black lacquered nail tapped against Mia's lapels. "If you want to save Ben, you need

176

to find a way to destroy the Nagas. We think there could be a way to achieve this using biological weapons. Congratulations, Mia. You're now the Lead Scientist of Project Sunflare."

So many thoughts and questions warred in Mia's head.

"I want you to get Ben off those drugs after the mission is over," said Mia, surprised at those words.

Fire flashed through Evelyn's eyes and a snarl twisted her lips. "How dare you make demands?"

Mia dropped the folder. "You need me."

"What we do for love." Evelyn widened her eyes in surprise. "Oh, he doesn't know. How typically male."

Mia felt her heart drop. Her voice quavered slightly as she said, "When Operation King Cobra is finished, he stops ingesting that crap."

Evelyn handed her back the folder. "Fine."

"Thank you."

Mia walked away, the folder clasped tightly in her hands. Just as she was about to exit the room, Evelyn's voice came from behind her.

"The EDF has never captured a live Naga specimen, you know," she said.

Mia stopped in her tracks. That was obvious. Why was she telling her that?

"But the Space Defense Force has. And that Naga is all yours once you get through that document. You have until tonight."

Chapter 18

Imperator

Nagaplex
15 December 2076
23:00

Imperator Kaali tried to hide the annoyance from his face as the Chief Scientist Vhaldie slithered before him and coiled his ugly, scaleless body. Not only did Vhaldie obstruct Kaali's view of the thousands of egg sacs that dangled from the top of the hatchery displaying their slowly reopening eggs, but Vhaldie also kept a too familiar proximity. And his eyes kept glancing at Saar, Kaali's daughter, who coiled behind her father.

"I am here to report on the strategy, Lord," said Vhaldie.

Back on their home world in Nagaloka, if Vhaldie approached Kaali with such familiarity in the Scaled Court he would've been whipped to death.

But Vhaldie had been the only one to come up with a solution against the egg sac disease that plagued their home world. An audacious solution that involved using the humans.

The scaleless belonged to the lower caste and wouldn't have dared to even glance at a royal of Imperator Kaali's pedigree. Yet the old retainer had slithered up Empress Nagini's ranks from a lowly hatchery keeper until he had become the Chief Scientist.

Nowadays Vhaldie was too valuable an asset to be punished whimsically.

"Saar, you go ahead and bless the egg sacs," Imperator Kaali spoke to his daughter who hid just behind him.

Today was Saar's coming of age ceremony and it coincided with her first fertility moon. Her beautiful glossy scales glowed from within, letting off a golden aura. Her sinuous hood displayed the intricate whorled pattern of Cobra Clan as she bowed. Burnished yellow eyes rimmed with black looked down and away from her father.

"Yes, Father," she said. She slid away.

Vhaldie's gray scaleless body with its splotchy yellow patterns slid his tail to the front, blocking Saar's passage.

"Stay for a moment, Princess Saar. I was just going to ask your father when our betrothal ceremony would take place?" Vhaldie said, his wide spaced eyes unblinking as he stared up at Kaali.

"Father, what is he—" asked Saar.

Imperator Kali said, "Go, now!"

Saar's hood flinched.

Vhaldie's tail slowly uncoiled, leaving a slim gap between the overhanging egg sacs and his own body, so that Saar was forced to brush past him.

Vhaldie openly stared at Saar's beautiful young body. His forked tongue flickered at the air. His greedy eyes widened.

Imperator Kaali hissed. A rage burned in him. If they were in their home world, he would've pounded Vhaldie into the ground. Empress Nagini be damned.

Vhaldie immediately turned his attention back to the Imperator and tightened into a coil, making him a smaller target.

"Sire, you promised—"

"You worm!" boomed Imperator Kaali. His hood flared open. His eyes widened. He hissed, baring his rows and rows of teeth. One venom spit and Vhaldie would turn into a slimy puddle. He restrained himself at the last moment and lashed out with his tail, using the sharp quills to scrape Vhaldie's face.

Vhaldie uttered a surprised yelp before twisting and tumbling to the side, crashing into the purple grass that provided a bed for the overhanging egg sacs.

Vhaldie stared back at Kaali. Three red scratch marks marred his face. They would never heal. Not from the tail quills of an Imperator.

Saar turned the corner and looked back. For a moment all three looked at one another.

"Keep going!" Kaali shouted at his daughter. He hated himself for being angry at her on such a special occasion. The guilt made him want to hack bile. He had not told her about the betrothal.

Back on their home world, there would have been a massive celebration.

Saar turned around the corner, disappearing amongst egg sacs and the purple fog.

Vhaldie's lips curled back in a snarl. His triangular-shaped head shaking with rage.

"You did not tell her," Vhaldie accused him.

Kaali controlled his breathing. He shouldn't have hit Vhaldie. When he lost control it reflected an uncertainty and turmoil within.

"My promise to the Empress will be kept." Kaali hissed, his jaws snapping. He found it extremely hard to say the next words. "You will be wed to my daughter after you've successfully hatched this batch of egg sacs. So I suggest you point your mind in that direction. If the humans attack us before the hatching our race will be extinct and we shall be doomed."

Vhaldie said, "Very well."

"Report, then," said the Imperator.

"After the last attack we lost a lot of our greens. And because of that there are too many blues out in the desert all gone crazed."

Each green Naga controlled a thousand blue Nagas. And if one of the green controllers died the thousand blues went insane.

"The humans had a good plan. They didn't expect us to have as many blues. You did well to hide them from view for all these years. They underestimated us." Imperator Kaali remembered the battle that started four months ago and lasted just as long. The humans had thrown wave after wave of themselves against the Nagaplex. And Imperator Kaali and his Nagas repelled every single wave.

But it had come too close and at a great price. They had lost almost all their green Nagas.

"The humans are planning another last desperate attack, called Operation King Cobra," said Vhaldie. "I've hatched four eggs prematurely. I have been experimenting

184

with them using my growth formula. I suggest we send them to pre-empt the humans attacking us."

Imperator Kaali shuddered as he recollected what Vhaldie had done to those four eggs. Those eggs were the first four eggs that hatched successfully in the last one hundred years. Their hatchlings looked sick and wasted. A part of Kaali was glad to be rid of them.

Kaali said, "We will send these experiments of yours right when the humans launch their mission. If we can destroy a single troop carrier that would mean thousands of human soldiers' lives."

"Yes, yes, I've given my darlings the ability to burrow deep within the earth. They will tunnel out from the center of the human base and wreak chaos."

As much as Kaali despised Vhaldie, nobody back in his home world could argue against the results. Everyone disagreed with Vhaldie's methods.

"Make sure they die. I don't want your experiments tainting our gene pool," said Kaali distastefully.

Vhaldie bowed his head. "Oh yes, they will die gloriously. After killing thousands of humans." He cackled. A drop of blood trickled down his eye. His forked tongue licked the blood away.

"Let's talk about the Nagaplex defenses. How many green Nagas do we have left?" Kaali asked.

"Ten."

"Is that all?" said Kaali. Even though that meant ten thousand blue Nagas still left for the green Nagas to mind command, it felt like a high risk.

"It will be enough after my four experiments wreak havoc on the humans' base," Vhaldie said with stiffness that bore of insubordination. Long ago Kaali would've squashed his neck.

But that was before Kaali had been placed on this mission to save the Naga race from extinction.

As Vhaldie slither-limped away, Imperator Kaali called out to him. "Vhaldie, when we have successfully repelled the next pitiful human attack, I will conduct the wedding ceremony. I will fulfill my promise to the Empress."

Vhaldie's forked tongue flickered into the air. "We shall destroy the humans. All of them."

Chapter 19

Laugh & Be Merry

Ben stood on Middle Hill and it had taken him a good one hour walk just to get there. He just had to get away from it all. He felt like he was going crazy. He was certain the neural helmet was messing with his brain. He kept thinking of other memories - places and things he'd never seen - but they felt real.

He walked up to the peak of the hill where a headstone sat amidst purple and white carnations. He wondered if whoever that headstone belonged to had committed suicide atop this hill. The gossip was rife among the new recruits that this is where everyone used to come to kill themselves.

A girl stood over the tombstone. She had long gold hair that caught the moonlight. He'd never seen her before.

"Hello?" he said.

The girl unfurled her back in a snakelike movement and turned to stare at him. She had golden eyes and skin that glimmered with vitality. She wore a beaded dress that hugged her form. She was tall, at least a full head taller than him.

"Greetings Earthling," she said.

Ben laughed. "Greetings Nagaling," he jokingly responded. "Are you from the air-force?"

She cocked her head slightly as if discerning a sound to which he couldn't readily hear. "I guess you could say that."

She walked up to him and pointed at the Naga bracelet he sported on his left hand. "I wanted to see you before I was promised to Vhaldie. I am the only survivor of my clan. And I must do as my father bids."

"Are you on the neural-helmet too?" He shook his head. "That stuff definitely makes you crazy." He patted his cloth bag. "I bought some snacks. Just got sick of it all. If you want to talk, we can sit on that bench."

Three pairs of stone benches edged the hill. Each pair consisted of two rows of stone benches split in the middle with a steelcrete table. Ben sat so that he could stare out into the base and watch all the activity. The girl sat alongside him.

He unzipped his cloth bag. "Here's the contraband. Cheez-It. Doritos. Rice Krispies. Fruit Gushers - did you know there were six flavors?" He opened the bags and laid them out on the table. He dug into the Chez-It box and grabbed out a handful which he held out to the girl. She seemed shy. "These are the best."

She held out her palms and he dropped the Cheeze-Its into them. Her eyebrows shot up at her first bite. "Fascinating."

"You must be from Australia? These are like American. I haven't had time to savor the Aussie sweets. They won't let us out of base."

"Ben, how do you feel about me?" she asked. And then before he could answer.

"You have been selected and I'm the only survivor of my clan."

Ben's heart jumped. The bracelet on his left hand glowed showing some type of words alongside it. It was Naga-script, but back then he didn't know. He stared at his bracelet and then at her. "Did you just do that?"

"I was just checking to make sure it was the right one. It would've been embarrassing if I had gotten to talk to somebody who had been aligned with a different clan."

Ben felt a sudden chill that had nothing to do with the gentle drizzle that started. "Wh-where are you from?"

That elegant neck turned and those golden eyes met his. She pointed up at two hundred billion galaxies - the sky plastered with glutinous stars - *I'm from space*, her gesture said.

"Really? Are you a Naga?" he said. He'd always been curious about Nagas. Unlike all the grunts in the base who just had rage to kill Nagas, Ben didn't feel that way. And Mia too. They both were just fascinated by them.

She nodded and held out her hands. Heptagonal scales glittered along her forearms. It wasn't a beaded dress, he realized. It was her skin. Was she some type of half Naga?

"I just really came to meet you. Our futures are intertwined. And… and I think I will need you to rescue me from Vhaldie," she said.

"What's your name?" he asked.

"Saar," she said.

"Saar," he pronounced. Saar, Saar, Saar, he said the word three times. "You have a Godly beauty about you. It's like somebody has made Enyo - the Greek goddess of war and brought her to life."

Saar laughed and it sounded like bells tinging against one another. "Enyo is not as powerful as me. But she is pretty."

"You know Enyo?" Ben asked. He loved Greek mythology. He'd studied it because he wanted to write a trilogy set in a world with Greek heroes. He shook his head. "Actually, don't answer that. I mean, what did you mean by you wanted to meet me? And what are these bracelets doing?"

Saar stood up suddenly like a King Cobra preparing to strike. Even though she bore no weapons he felt she was just as dangerous as General Katana.

"Ten people are approaching," she said, standing up with an air of finality.

Ben reached out to shake her hand. She tilted her head quizzically took his hand and brought it to her lips where she breathed upon his knuckles. He felt a flutter of cold kisses across his collarbone. "I'm glad that my father chose you. Your heart sees true and your soul is bright and filled with virtue."

Saar turned and walked into the night. Her body twisted as if she became a 2D image and then she melted into the dark.

Ben heard the footsteps coming up the path and grabbed all the junk food he laid out and quickly squashed it into his cloth bag. He rolled to the ground and crab crawled under a bush.

Just in time.

General Katana and Chief Admiral Evelyn Wilson walked up the pathway that lead to the headstone. Behind them hulking bodyguards spread out in a protective zone. One of the brutes stood only a step away from Ben, but he was so submerged in the bush and utterly still that the bodyguard didn't notice.

Am I dreaming this all? Or is this real? He wondered. Wearing that neural cap thingy made him feel all fuzzy in the head sometimes.

ૐ

Chief Admiral Evelyn Wilson, one of the most powerful person's in the planet, hesitated as she stood outside that door. She almost turned back as uncertainty snaked into her mind. She shook her head as if dispelling the uncertainty and raised her hand. Knock. Knock. Knock. She could have swiped her hand across the door's sensor and it would've scanned her dog tag and immediately opened.

But she did not.

She waited there until the voice came from within.

"Enter," said the firm voice. Even the voice held a level of confidence in its sheer clarity, tone, and diction. *Come right in and dare to face me,* said the underlying words.

The chief swallowed and the door opened wish a swish revealing a spartan office room that belonged to the most powerful person in the Earth Defense Force's history: General Onna Bugeisha Katana. Onna to Evelyn. To everyone else: General Katana.

Evelyn walked into the room. She didn't accuse Onna of ignoring her three calls and three emails.

"It's Rose's birthday today," said Evelyn.

"Lyn, you know I don't have time to celebrate birthdays," said Onna. She stood by her desk which had eight holograms displaying battle plans. Each plan a variation of the original plan. The words 'Operation King Cobra' hovered over the main display.

"Onna, it is our daughter's death anniversary. We vowed to do this every year. To remember her," said Evelyn. The general continued to frown at the displays and she reached out to swipe on a military unit to reposition it and then replayed the simulation.

Evelyn reached out and slammed the 'off' button that sat against the desk. The eight displays vanished in a flash of light that sucked into the miniature projectors inbuilt in the desk.

"I told you I didn't want to see you anymore…" The general's glowing artificial eye dimmed as she turned away. Her silver spiky hair now plastered itself against her scalp. She looked tired and old beyond her time. Turning off the display was like ripping the drapes that covered the secrets of a magical act and exposed the truth to the audience.

"I'm not here to see you," Evelyn lied. "I'm here to pay respects to our daughter's grave. Together. As you promised." She felt so lonely without Onna and her daughter. Never in a million years did Evelyn Wilson think she would be *that* person. Her career at the Space Defense Force kept her sane.

"That was ten years ago." Onna wiped her face. She stood much taller now with the artificial feet given to her after her battle with the Nagas left her a paraplegic.

Onna had dragged her torso for a hundred miles using her hands. That was one of the many myths surrounding General Katana. These days it was hard to tell which were false or true.

"You promised," said Evelyn.

Onna walked around the table. Her robotic feet made the sound of blades slicing against the air. She was a head taller than Evelyn. "You always knew what to say."

But Onna made her way to the door, turned, and looked at Evelyn. "Coming?" She stood there with her large arms clasped behind her back. The urban camouflage sleeveless vest displayed her biceps now decorated with ten black lines representing the Naga's she killed. Evelyn remembered biceps empty of such gruesome markers.

Evelyn strode out of the room and snaked her hand through the gap in Onna's arm. She stared at her ex-lover defiantly.

Onna huffed, her mouth opened about to say something, but then it remained shut. They both walked out of the Earth Defense Force administrative offices with eight elite soldiers surrounding them: four Black Berets and four Space Marines.

The sky took on a dark hue and a slight drizzle kissed the faces of Evelyn and Onna as they made their way up Middle Hill. Their eight bodyguards disappeared in the clingy fog. The grassy hill perched up high in the middle of Capital Base Oceania and overlooked the entire base. A newly erected chain linked fence with tiger wire surrounded the perimeter of the hill. White signs tied to the fence at ten foot intervals repeated the same thing: *Your Country Needs You. Suicide Is A Coward's Out. Fight For Humanity. Kill Nagas.*

"It has cut the suicides down by seventy percent," said Onna, nodding at the signs as she strode up the path with Evelyn's hand stuck in the crook of her elbow.

"I have the same problems. They were spacing themselves from airlocks, so I put on multiple levels of authorization required to use the airlocks," said Evelyn.

Tiny yellow lights edged the stone path that lead to the only headstone perched at the very edge of the cliff like some type of ominous warning sign. Freshly cut grass filled the air with a sweet smell.

The various sounds of the base could still be heard from here, though somewhat faint. Large hangars filled with Predator mechs being machined and prepped for the Space Defense Force sat just a few hundred feet away from the cliff face.

The two leaders came to a stop a foot away from the headstone. Evelyn removed her arm from Onna's and squatted on the ground so that she was at eye level with the top of the headstone.

Private Rose Bugeisha-Wilson (2056-2075)
~ Gone Too Soon ~
Operation Nightstorm

Three rows of carnations cascaded down from the headstone. Purple petals with white centers oozed out a sweet smell.

Evelyn looked up at Onna. "Thanks for keeping the flowers alive."

Onna knelt down. She looked like an avenging angel from hell with her robotic legs, silver hair, and glowing beady eye. "The Nagas will pay."

"Remember what she said to us? Her favorite poem." *Forget about the enemy for now*, thought Evelyn.

"Happy nineteenth, Rose, I miss you every single day," said Onna, a tear slid down her right cheek. Scarred fingers covered her face.

Evelyn took a deep breath and recited their daughter's favorite poem:

Laugh and be merry, remember, better the world with a song,

Better the world with a hug in the teeth of a wrong.

Laugh, for the time is brief, a day the length of a blink.

Laugh and be proud to belong to the old pageant of mankind.

And Evelyn kept reciting the poem, even through the sob that tore itself from Onna's mouth like the anguished wail of someone dying, even through her own tears that blurred her vision and through her own pain that could never be salvaged.

Chapter 20

AMROF

Advanced Map Reading and Objective
Following (AMROF)
Kangaroo Forest
31 December 2076
18:00

1 st Foot Soldier Battalion, all one hundred thousand soldiers, divided themselves into ten, and that was further divided into ten, and the last one thousand soldiers occupied the east side of the

ginormous base—which was more like an entire state—to carry out the AMROF exercise.

Groups of kids now in their assigned squads clumped all over the orientation area, which was designed to resemble the terrain in the 'Graveyard'—the desert-like perimeter around the Nagaplex.

For the members of Alpha One Tango—Zhi, Ben, Jadyn, and Natalie—this resulted in a complete blow-up during an orienteering exercise in which the squad needed to decipher markers on a map. The exercise focused on developing a clear sense of direction when dropped into enemy territory.

The kicker being that the squads had been calorie restricted—or as Ben preferred to call it 'starved'—the prior forty-eight hours. This simulated exact battlefield conditions in a prior operation.

Ben wanted to rip out his hair in frustration. He hadn't been sleeping well since the first day he joined. He felt constantly amped. He would've done so if the infantry hadn't forced a buzz cut on him. Ripped out his hair strand by strand and screamed in frustration.

"You've gotta be kidding!" shouted Jadyn. "It's obviously that way. You can't read a basic map." His thick fingers ripped the map out of Ben's hands.

Whatever was in those purple vials had transformed Jadyn's body over the last month. Ben couldn't recognize Jadyn from the day he got here. The puppy fat was gone. His muscles corded and rippled along his forearms. His chin was cleanly cut, revealing sharp edges. But he looked older too, and Ben swore he could see gray at the sides of his temples.

Ben closed his eyes and pressed his fingers against the side of his head. Recently he'd been getting migraines. They happened randomly. A dose of gym-candy cured it—that's what the kids called the purple vials of growth hormone.

Ben fumbled at the storage section within his belt. It opened with a hiss, revealing the last purple vial. He grabbed it with a sigh, rolled up his sleeves, and plunged it in. Ice cold shot up his veins and into his head. The pounding headache instantly died down.

"Your last dose is meant to be at 2200 hours," Zhi said. "Not now."

"I can't, migraines…" Ben stammered out the words. For a moment the world swam before his eyes.

Zhi lunged at him and grabbed his collar. She shook him. "Hey, do that again and I'll eject you from this squad. That dosage pattern has to be followed exactly."

The world still swam in front of Ben's eyes.

"Do you understand?!" Zhi screamed, shaking him.

"Yes, yes, squad leader," Ben said. *Why is she so upset?* he thought.

Zhi turned around and addressed them all. "If anybody takes a dosage of the growth hormone a second before or after the recommended times, I will have you ejected from this squad."

Jadyn and Natalie looked up from crouching on the floor. Zhi's anger hit them like a palpable force. "Sure," they both echoed.

Ejection was the worst thing anyone could imagine. A society grown up on Earth Defense Force mandates shunned soldiers who failed. An ejected soldier lived a lonely life of alcoholism, depression, and suicide.

Zhi appeared to gather herself. She took a deep breath. "Where are we?"

"Lost," said Jadyn.

"We can't be. We've been marching for two hours. We should've hit what that map descriptions says," Ben said.

"Welcome to Advanced Map Orientation!" Andy shouted from beyond the hill. "Where you get to run around circles all day long with a bunch of clueless kids." He was actually the squad leader for his own squad and right now they were lost, too.

Matt and his own squad were in the valley below them and they were also consulting their maps. Everyone was lost. Matt raised up his hand upwards in the universal gesture of 'who knows?' and turned back to reading his map.

They had thirteen hours to get to their location.

It had been twelve hours already and now tempers were bursting.

One hour left.

"Ben, we've been following your clueless directions for the last two hours," said Jadyn. He pointed a finger at Natalie. "And we've tried your ideas too."

They stood in a mountainous region with forest to their left and right. An off-road trail made of orange rocks went up the mountain.

They carried backpacks with food, water, and shelter. Their webbing held their ammunition and their M18's made a heavy weight on their arms. And to make it worse the big black flies kept biting them.

Ben had never seen such big black flies before. He kept swatting them away. If he didn't, they landed and bit at him *through* his clothes.

Zhi looked up at Natalie. "What about you? Are you giving up so easily? You are part of this squad too."

Ben wondered why Zhi intimidated Natalie. Only later did he realize Zhi's leadership genius. She sought out the thoughts of everyone in her squad. It made the squad better, and when Zhi didn't know enough on her own she relied on other perspectives to guide her decisions. She also believed in positive pressure.

Natalie swallowed. She hardly spoke during the squad exercises. Most of the time it was Ben, Jadyn, and Zhi. "What if the description on the map is fake? Or incorrect?"

Zhi's eyebrows rose delicately.

"Conspiracy theories? Screw me alive," said Jadyn.

"Shut up," said Zhi. The look she gave Jadyn made him back down. "Go on," Zhi said to Natalie.

Jadyn turned away and bounced on his feet. He muttered to himself.

Twelve hours of marching with no food and now no water—they'd just used the last of it up an hour ago. But Jadyn was still amped. Ben was edgy. Jadyn kept mumbling to himself and slamming a fist into his palm.

Natalie said, "Um, I was thinking maybe the descriptions are wrong. For example—" Zhi stepped to Natalie's side and held the map so Natalie could read it. "Um, an old tank sits to the left of Mount Speculation. But we did follow the directions and there were no tanks. Um, we turned back because we didn't see the tank."

"Because we were heading in the wrong damn direction!" said Jadyn.

"Jadyn, Natalie hasn't finished." Zhi's unblinking stare found his.

Jadyn mumbled, "Whatever," and glanced away.

"Natalie, you need to get to the point. Time," said Ben. She was all over the place. For the first few weeks happy but now it was a complete turnaround. She always spoke in the most torturous fashion. Also she never kept eye contact.

Natalie would later on reveal the details of her past to her squad and from then on Ben and Jadyn stopped teasing her.

"Go on, Natalie," said Zhi, giving Ben a glare.

"I think we were heading the right way," said Natalie. "Those descriptions are wrong. I think this goes back to the lesson General Katana was talking about. Of being aware. When we get dropped to face the Nagas in two months' time, we are going to need to be self-aware. The terrain out there is chaotic. The Nagas switch up landmarks to confuse humans on purpose. Each one of General Katana's exercises has had a deeper meaning to them."

Jadyn jumped up and down. "I have nightmares about those exercises. So let's say you're on to something."

Natalie's index finger tapped against the map in the spot where they had been previously. "I think that's where we need to head back to. We were right at the beginning. We just didn't believe it because of those descriptions."

"Why didn't you open your mouth then?" asked Jadyn.

Natalie averted his gaze.

"Because nobody gave her the chance," said Zhi. Her stare had no effect on Jadyn this time.

"She should speak the frig up," said Jadyn. "We are the damn EDF and we're going to face Nagas. I for one don't want a squad member who's afraid to speak up."

"She just spoke up," said Zhi. "And what she had to say made a lot of sense."

The sun set across the horizon, bathing the sky in a purple orange that signified the coming of the night. Ben suddenly felt so small and insignificant with his squad in that bush land. Surrounded by the occasional tall, blackened trees. But all around them was the red desert. Its barren, cracked surface looked never-ending.

"Ben?" asked Zhi.

Ben realized she had been talking to him.

"Yes?"

"Do you agree it makes sense?"

"Yep, makes sense," he said.

"What makes sense?" Zhi asked.

Ben shook his head. What had they been talking about? Memories deserted him suddenly and a deep blackness enveloped him. What was going on with him?

"Focus." Zhi tapped on his forehead. "Natalie was saying we head back east. If we are going to make it in time, we're going to have to dump our packs. Otherwise we'll be disqualified."

"Hell yeah," said Jadyn. He unslung his backpack and dumped it to the ground.

They dumped their packs and proceeded with haste to the location on the map.

It turned out Natalie was right.

From then on Ben decided he would ask Natalie what she was thinking every single time.

Chapter 21

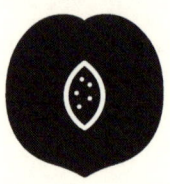

My Sweet Peach

Two months ago…

Family Day
New York, The Bronx
30 November 2076
20:00

On Family Day when all the kids all around the world enjoyed the last day they would get to have hang out with their families, Natalie's heart filled with fear as she stood outside her own home.

The box-shaped apartment stared back at her from under a constantly flickering light. The passageway that connected the apartments filled with junk, puddles of water, and the odd crack addict. Behind her a cold wind blew across The Bronx and the moonlight cast a dim glow on the larger than usual crowd that braved the dark.

Natalie's hand trembled and fell back down as she reached out to put it against the square door sensor with the blinking red light. Apartment number 1303.

Television sounds came from within. The fight between Oscar Rouso and Shania Calloway bled out through the smeared windows and forlorn curtains. A chilling breeze lifted the curtain and revealed a glimpse of the interior.

A long, dark silhouette lounged on the chair in front of the huge display. Occasionally, it would take a sip of beer from a can, gulp at it, crush it, and fling it to the ground.

Dad.

Run away, she told herself. *Just turn and run. You only have one day left—he won't find you. Tomorrow is Earth Defense Force Orientation Day. All you have to do is survive one night out in the cold.*

Natalie turned around to evaluate her chances. "Where would I go?" she said to herself. Could she escape him, finally?

Yellow watery light flared from stark lampposts. The lone gray cloud cut itself against the sickle moon. A howl pierced the night. It drizzled when she left school and hadn't stopped. The rain pattered behind her, marking the gray stone.

Natalie's apartment sat at the end of a bunch of apartments.

Dad preferred it that way.

"He will come for me." Fear made her turn back to face her house. He would find her. He always did.

Confront your fears, Natalie. She squeezed her eyes tight and quickly swiped across the door sensor. It beeped and the door shuddered open, the rubber lining old and frayed.

The house smelled of beer. Crushed aluminum cans lay in random piles, occasionally glinting against the light from the TV. A rat scurried against the edge of the wall holding an orange Cheeto in its mouth. It disappeared beneath a gap between the floorboards. The stench of unflushed toilet came from the left of the kitchen.

As soon as Natalie stepped inside, the light from the TV switched off. The noise of boxing and rowdy spectators plunged away, leaving the apartment in sudden silence.

The dark silhouette that stretched itself in front of the TV pooled like liquid ink and began to stand. It turned Natalie's way.

Ice-cold fear shot through Natalie as her father's sunken cheeks and hollow eyes gazed at her. His too-wide jaw dotted itself in gray. Large yellow teeth smiled. The eyes shadowed under overhanging eyebrows.

His feet shuffled forward like a zombie.

"My sweet peach," he said. His sandpaper voice grazed the skin at the back of her neck. The stench of death and decay came with him as he stopped in front of her.

Hands like pliers gripped her chin and tilted her face up to stare into his black pits.

"It's your last day at home," he said. "My sweet peach is going to join the EDF tomorrow and become a big powerful soldier. Are you looking forward to that?" His other hand gripped the top of Natalie's red hair and suddenly slammed her head back into the wall.

The pain ricocheted through the back of Natalie's skull. If she didn't answer him it would get worse for her. Some part of her, a small, insignificant part that hadn't caved into hopelessness, that small part made her say the words she would regret.

"Yes." Then with a greater surety. "Yes!"

Dad backhanded her. The world twisted in Natalie's eyes and the floor came up to smack her against the side of her head. She didn't have time to reach. She screamed as he pulled at her hair, dragging her along. She screamed even higher as she realized he was taking her to his bedroom.

Daddy raped her over and over again.

He only stopped when the tiredness and the alcohol turned him into a barely breathing husk. Compared to all the other times he had taken her, tonight had been the worst. She thought he might not stop.

Natalie sat naked on the bed. Her body a painting of red slashes across a pale canvas. Her finger trembled as she sniffed and wiped the snot away.

The clock struck 0700 hours. It was Earth Defense Force Orientation Day.

Natalie stood up and headed to her room. She didn't dare use the shower that reeked of filth and scum. Her hands shook as she took the wet tissues from a dispenser. She wiped the stink of her father from her body. She wiped away the blood. She wiped at the tears.

Her reflection stared back at her from the cracked mirror. The vertical marks across her pale arms went from her wrists to her shoulders. She even sported a pale scar just above her neck. She turned away abruptly. *Why, God? Why me?*

Natalie tore open the plastic bag that housed her Earth Defense Force uniform. She put on the top and then the pants and then the boots. She made sure the cap stayed low, covering the bruises across her face.

Natalie left her home and didn't look back.

Chapter 22

Project Sunflare

Space Station
17 December 2076
21:00

The International Space Station—
Space Defense Force, ISS-SDF,
consisted of two giant wheels connected via a huge cylindrical central hub.
Four spokes stretched out from either end
of the hub to connect to the outer rim of
each wheel.

The space station floated at Lagrange Point Five, 384,400 kilometers from Earth, at a scientifically established location in which gravitational forces allowed a parked object. The space station followed Earth's orbital pattern.

Sixty-one thousand Space Defense Force personnel called the ISS-SDF home. Those SDF divisions included the Armed Wing, Strategic Space Command, Astro Science, and Planetfall Troopers.

From a huge window that stretched out from the executive office of Strategic Space Command, at the highest level of the central hub, Chief Admiral Evelyn Wilson put her hands against the balcony railing and stared out into space at the Naga wormhole.

That wormhole had been there for over ten years, ever since the Nagas invaded Earth, and had been dormant ever since. Indeed, that was the precursor that put the construction of the ISS-SDF into overdrive, and within a year of the Naga invasion this space station became fully operational.

Yet, it wasn't the dormant wormhole that attracted the Chief's eyes. Not today at least. Instead it was the presence of a diminutive young girl, the youngest ever recruit to be admitted to the Space Defense Force, who sat on a seat nervously staring up at the Chief's face.

"You're certain of this, Mia?" asked the Chief.

"Yes, Chief," replied Mia.

"Forget about the formality. This is the Space Defense Force, not the Earth Defense Force." She crossed her arms and it made the medals on her lapels glow. "Call me Evelyn." The Chief turned and walked back to her large antique mahogany desk. She typed on her keyboard and said, "This is Chief Admiral Evelyn Wilson. I would like a priority call with General Katana."

"Connecting to Earth, Australia," said the computer.

"Come stand here," said the Chief.

Mia stood up from the seat she occupied at the end of the huge table and headed toward the Chief Admiral. The older woman stood in front of the huge window. The window darkened and turned completely black before a figure slowly appeared.

The face of General Katana stared at them from a display that stretched across the entire wall. Sweat beaded her forehead and she sported a frown.

"What is it, Evelyn?" said General Katana.

The sounds of guns firing filled the room, causing Mia to jump. It came from the General's end.

"One of my scientists discovered something about the Nagaplex. I want you to hear about it firsthand." Evelyn beckoned Mia. "This is Special Projects Lead Scientist Mia Johnson-Patel. She's in our Astro Science division."

"Hold up," said the General. She turned and sprinted away from the noise. When she stopped a huge hangar bay sat in the background.

"What did she discover?" asked the General.

"That the Nagaplex is alive," said Evelyn.

Mia expected a challenge. She's encountered many objections in her own division when she first announced her discovery three weeks back. Eventually, Mia got the chance to present irrefutable proof.

But General Katana didn't ask for irrefutable proof.

"Very well. It has come to this. Are we on the same page?" asked the General.

Chief Admiral Evelyn Wilson nodded. "Biological Weapons."

"Which could backfire and kill my soldiers."

"You were the one who pushed me for a solution. This is what we have."

"How?"

"Detonation. Basically, mix the biological weapons with our latest bombs. Send a squad in there to plant it and detonate it remotely."

"Do we have time to test this?" asked the general.

"No," replied Evelyn.

"The risk—"

"—is that we become extinct as a species," finished Evelyn. "It is a soldier's job to die for her country. These soldiers are dying for the sake of the planet."

"Easy for you to say, sitting up there in space," said the General. "You get all the funding to build spacecraft carriers while I get recycled rations."

Evelyn's face reddened.

The General held up her hand. "I apol-ogize." Her slender fingers filled with scars covered her face. When she looked back up, a watery glint filled her eyes. "You have two months to get the weapon to me." The display darkened and vanished.

Mia and Evelyn were left looking out into the darkness of space.

Evelyn gave a dejected sigh. She turned to Mia. "What's the progress with Project Sunflare?"

"About thirty percent finished. But what's this—"

"Project Sunflare is a weapons project. You didn't figure that out?"

Mia felt her stomach sink. She'd been too focussed on studying the Nagas. The chemistry. Making the plan and getting the right resources on board. It hit her like a brick to the head.

Evelyn's mouth quirked. "Well, let me be clear. Start working with your team to develop a biological agent that can kill the Nagaplex."

Chapter 23

Collateral Damage

Battlefield #5
30 December 2076
15:00

"Today is a live fire exercise. This is the Mongoose 18, or as we call it back at home the M18. It is by far the most reliable weapon against the Nagas. We retrieved the dog tags from all the downed soldiers in Operation Python and were able to harness their experiences. The M18 was by far the most effective weapon they used." Sergeant Clinton smiled at them as he strode to the Wild-Boar Jeep and jumped on the back of it.

The sergeant continued, "Combined with the accelerated learning that you're doing thanks to the wonderful neural helmets, and the massive physical gains thanks to our homemade organic growth-soup, you might all live well past the sixty seconds after being deployed on the LZ."

Some nervous laughter arose from the assembled recruits. Twenty-five squads stood in one of the many mock battle-fields that scattered themselves around the capital base. Cactus, tumble brush, and the occasional rock graced the red, cracked sand. A lone Earth Defense Force flag fluttered in the middle of the battle-field atop a hill surrounded by sandbags.

Ben stared at his squad, Alpha One Tango, and marveled at the changes that had occurred in the last two months. Natalie had lost the double chin. A clear resoluteness appeared in her green eyes. She'd toned in ways Ben found surpris-ing. And embarrassing, considering they all showered in the same bathroom.

Zhi looked like a lizard on juice. She was already lean when she arrived. Now she was leaner. She was already strong when she arrived. Now she was much stronger. It scared him how quick she was in Naga-jitsu sparring sessions.

And Jadyn, he'd taken to the growth hormone the best. He resembled a Zulu warrior. The muscles practically popped out of his frame. They had to give him a specially designed uniform to fit his six-foot-eight frame. He was huge and strong.

Sergeant Clinton stood at the back of one of the Wild-Boar Jeeps. His left knee rested on the gunner platform. The two long barrels pointed up in the air behind him. He said, "There is only one rule: this is a free for all. No cooperation between squads."

"I've done this before," Jadyn blurted out, before realizing he said it aloud. Memories flashed through him. Sometimes he thought he could see people following him out the corner of his eye. "And something bad happened." He looked down at his feet and mumbled to himself.

"What do you mean?" asked Zhi.

"Do you guys get random flashbacks?" asked Ben. "I could strip this baby and put it apart like I've been doing it my whole life. I know which way Nagas like to feint. I even think I know parts of Operation Python." He held out the M18.

"Not flashbacks," said Natalie. "But sometimes...I feel like I'm somebody else when I put on that neural helmet." She laughed self-deprecatingly. "Must just be crazy me."

Jadyn, Zhi, and Ben stared at one another. They all noticed small discrepancies and brushed them off. There wasn't any time. When Zhi had asked about side effects, the entire squad received an email from Combat Stress Control medical attachment saying their symptoms were due to stress.

"Ooorah!" Sergeant Clinton shouted. "Let's begin."

Jadyn muttered to himself. "We got them, Mike. I'll cover you." His eyes glazed and he shook himself.

Ben wondered who the heck was Mike.

"Squad on me," Zhi called out loudly. "This is a live fire exercise. Keep your helmets on and dial them to full."

They wore their full-body armor with the transformable helmet. The helmet could be configured with two different levels: full and half. At full configuration the visor covered the eyes and the helmet extended to cover the lower jaw. At half configuration the helmet retracted the visor and lower jaw protection, leaving the face exposed.

Ben clicked the two buttons in the side of his helmet, shutting down his visor. When Zhi spoke next her voice came in on the squad channel, out of the helmet's speakers.

"Hey!" Zhi shouted.

Jadyn turned around. He'd already left before Zhi gave out the squad instructions.

"What?" Jadyn asked.

"Instructions," Zhi said. "On me."

"You already gave them," said Jadyn.

"Come back, I've got new ones," said Zhi.

That confused Ben. Zhi never gave the first instructions. He shared a glance with Natalie. She shrugged.

All around them the other squads were already taking their positions. The battlefield was purposely small to force confrontation. There were two other squads on either side of Alpha One Tango.

Jadyn's harsh breathing filled the air as Zhi gave them her instructions. Zhi's plan was a defensive one and had them going for cover.

"That's not going to do it," said Jadyn. "We'll be killed. We need to go straight for the flag. Those Nagas will feint left."

"What do you think?" Zhi asked Natalie.

Natalie licked her lips. Her eyes darted to the towering Jadyn and back to Zhi. "Twenty-five other squads. We should run for it."

Gunfire hit the air and they all immediately turned. Ben ducked low on his stomach. In the distance somebody's body jerked like a puppet as it got shot. The firing stopped once the person went down. The full-body armor could take three shots from an M18 before damage. The rule of the exercise was that one shot and you had to lie down.

"Ben, what about you?" Zhi asked.

A turned-over tank provided cover. They all lay on the ground, protecting each other from fire and positioning themselves in a manner that enabled them to provide suppressing. The red, cracked earth filled the horizon. Soldiers moved over the horizon like ghosts.

"We're going to die if we stay put," Ben said. Only that's not what he meant to say. Those words came out of his mouth from somebody else's memories. He shook his head.

"Cheerful," said Natalie.

"Shit!" Zhi said.

Jadyn's huge, towering form ran across the horizon. He skidded to a halt and fired. His M18 cracking at the air. An entire enemy squad went after him.

Zhi sprinted after Jadyn.

"Let's go!" Ben shouted to Natalie.

Everything happened in a blur of speed. Gunfire, the flash of lights, screams. Exploding grenades. Ben hated it. He gritted his teeth and pounded after Zhi.

"Ben!" Natalie screamed.

Ben fell on his stomach with his M18 held out right in front of him. He fired without even thinking. Rolled to his left. Fired again.

Natalie worked in synch with him, firing in between Ben's rolls, providing support.

Six bodies lay comatose around them.

Smoke and the acidic stench of the M18's bullets filled the air. Ben's breathing sounded harsh in his helmet. He wanted badly to open the visor but knew Zhi would have his balls. It was so hot.

"Clear," said Natalie. "But…shit, there's Jadyn!" Natalie jumped up and ran.

The red battlefield up ahead filled with pockets of smoke and the downed bodies of soldiers. A partially demolished building had been used for cover, and fighting there had been concentrated. Bodies littered everywhere. A huge set of footsteps cut through this destruction, leaving massive marks in the red sand. Following Jadyn was like following a T-Rex.

"The flag," said Ben. He couldn't believe they'd made it this far. "We've made it to the flag. How the heck is that possible?" He kept checking the horizon through the sights on his M18.

Natalie mirrored his exact checks on the other side as they walked side by side up the hill.

The first thing Ben noticed was the blood on top of the hill. A dozen bodies lay at the base of the flagpole. They were twisted and bent.

"They aren't playing dead…" Ben crunched to his knees. "What's happened?"

Zhi's small form stood there with her head bent.

Jadyn knelt on the floor. A torturous scream rent the air. The big kid raised both his hands in the air and shouted, "Why?"

A young black kid with his helmet torn off lay on the ground in front of Jadyn. The dead kid's head cracked with a huge hole oozing blood. He looked like a dead doll.

"Denzel," Jadyn screamed. "Denzel!" He howled into the air like a wolf.

Natalie whispered to Ben. "Who is Denzel?"

Ben pointed. "That dead kid."

Natalie shook her head. "That's Chris."

Four medics flanked Sergeant Clinton as he strode up the hill. His face drained of color. "Jadyn," he said. "Jadyn, I need you to listen to me."

The big kid's shoulders slumped. "Denzel's dead." Jadyn threw his helmet to the ground. His red-rimmed eyes stared around wildly. He brought up his M18 and aimed it at Sergeant Clinton. "You gave the order!"

But the sergeant fired before Jadyn could pull his trigger. A bullet slammed into Jadyn's neck, taking him down.

Ben screamed as he fell down on his knees, reaching for Jadyn. He lunged for Sergeant Clinton, wrapping his hands around his neck. The sergeant backhanded him with the butt of his rifle. Ben absorbed the blow against his own rifle and let it fall to the ground. He used the only weapon he had: his teeth. He chomped down on the sergeant's neck.

And then blackness took him.

General Katana's AI audio log. Recorded conversation between herself and Chief Admiral Evelyn Wilson.

START/

"Side effects were not meant to kick in so quickly. It's only been two months."

"His younger brother stole his older brother's identity. Identity swap in this case, not identity theft. He died two years ago. The NPR must've kicked something neurologically in Jadyn. For some reason he thought that kid he killed was his younger brother. The kid he killed was Chris Kennedy."

"Will this happen again? Fifty recruits were killed."

"You're asking me? Speak of the Devil, indeed. We're giving these kids a cocktail of Naga Growth Hormone and Neural Pathway Reconditioning and the strongest dosages of both. We are reaping what we sowed."

"You don't understand. The way he killed those kids matched the way a previous multi homicide occurred in Operation Python. It was like Jadyn downloaded memories of a previous soldier and then replicated the exact actions."

"That…shouldn't be possible. But I will check."

"You took all our resources to build your scientific empire. And that's what you're giving me?"

"You asked my scientists to give them NGH version J. That was ten years of physical soldier conditioning in three months. Jadyn is a genetic freak. His reaction to the growth hormone is unparalleled. We need to study this kid in our labs."

"What I need to know is, will he flip again?"

"You made him into Hulk with a trigger that we can't identify. Keep pointing him at the Nagas."

"Many are showing the listed side effects. I'm hoping they can last one month longer."

"Humanity rests on that hope."

/END

Chapter 24

The Washingtons

Two years ago…

New York, Staten Island
21 February 2074
13:00

Denzel came up with the idea two years ago. Jadyn's younger brother was one of the smartest kids he'd ever known. Denzel didn't go to normal school. He suffered from autism and epilepsy. He went to a special school. He spent all his time on the dark net when he got home.

Two years ago, Jadyn had been in his final year of high school. The draft would kick in. He would be sent to the infantry and that meant certain death.

That's the day Denzel had come up with the idea.

"Jadyn?" Denzel asked, peeking into his older brother's bedroom.

"Sup bro?" Jadyn said, throwing his tablet to the ground. "Come in." He rested on his bed, reading comics.

His younger brother sat at the foot of the bed and stared down at the tablet. "Naga Slayer Issue Five!" Denzel said, picking it up and reading it.

Denzel loved staring at the pictures. Jadyn patiently let him read the entire comic before gently taking the tablet away. Denzel didn't like anybody touching him. So Jadyn made sure he took the tablet away from Denzel's hands without touching him.

"What's up, my man?" Jadyn asked.

"You will get drafted. Sent to infantry. Die," said Denzel. Each time he said a word his eyes flicked to Jadyn and then back down. "I love you."

"I love you too," said Jadyn. It was the first time anybody said those words to him. He wiped at his tears. "I could survive," he said. He didn't believe it. Everyone knew that an infantry soldier dropped into a Naga-infested LZ only had sixty seconds to live.

Denzel looked into Jadyn's eyes suddenly. His face lost the constant apprehensive look. At that moment his younger brother looked mature and confident.

"I know a way to let you live," said Denzel.

"How?" Jadyn asked.

"I can hack into the EDF database. Change your graduation year and date of birth by two years," said Denzel.

Jadyn couldn't help the smile that split his face. "Really?"

Denzel nodded. "Of course."

Jadyn surged forward and hugged his brother. Denzel stiffened. Jadyn was about to apologize for touching him, but then Denzel returned the hug.

They both stood up and jumped around Jadyn's room laughing.

"Thank you, Denzel," Jadyn said. "Thank you!"

It was only later that Jadyn realized what Denzel had done. He had hacked into the Earth Defense Force database and swapped their names. So Denzel got drafted first.

To the horror of Jadyn and his father.

His younger brother had gone to war before him and died. He had given Jadyn two years to figure out a way out of the system.

Jadyn never did.

Chapter 25

Agent Yellow

Space Station
20 December 2076
06:30

The red Naga hissed, its huge head towering into the air. Its hood flared and its huge, gaping jaws opened, revealing a cavernous throat serrated with sharp teeth. It spat viscous venom that sizzled into the air and headed right for Mia's head.

The venom splattered against the four-foot-thick reinforced glass panels and ate into the first three panes of glass, completely melting it.

Knowing blue eyes stared at Mia.

If Mia didn't have the protection of the reinforced glass panels, she would've been human goop by now. Six other scientists from the Astro Science division filled the laboratory. Three of them had joined the Space Defense Force three years before Mia, but in this particular experiment they'd been designated as Mia's assistants. The other scientist being Mia's boss, Biology Director Ray Martinez, and the last person was strictly not a scientist but was present today because of the importance of the occasion: Chief Admiral Evelyn Wilson, dressed in lab whites.

"How long will the glass last before we need to replace it?" asked the Chief.

"Long enough for us to finish our experiment, which is in the next three minutes," answered Ray. He wiped sweat from his brow. "You're good?"

"Don't talk to her. We don't want her distracted," said the Chief.

Mia was glad for the Chief's words. Her boss was an annoying micro-manager. It would be better if he just got out of the way. Her eyes met the Chief's and she nodded.

Mia's hands enclosed themselves in the robotic actuator gloves within the micro-gravity science glove box, a large square panel with glass on one side and two holes that Mia inserted her arms into—actuator arms. They protected her from radiation, amplified strength, and enabled nanometer-level precision.

Her left hand held a vial that over-flowed with a smoky substance. Her right-hand robotic glove had a ring-like clasp at the end of each finger that held five vials. The vials glistened with condensation and their tops brimmed in a yellowish hue. A slender sticker on each of the vials said: 'Sarin Unmodified.'

"I'm about to modify the sarin with my pyro-oil, testing each one by one nanometer to see which one gets the correct yield," she said to her diary recorder. The computer in the room tracked and recorded her experiment.

Mia's nerves reached a peak because this was her one hundredth attempt at doing this. She'd failed ninety-nine times previously.

She held her breath as she mixed a nanometer of pyro-gel with the sarin. Her plan was to increment by a nanometer per vial. One nanometer on the first vial, two on the second, until she reached five.

In the first vial, she mixed the sarin with five nanometers of pyro-gel. It disintegrated almost immediately. She ignored the feeling of despair within her and went on to the next one. Each one disintegrated almost immediately. She stopped breathing when she mixed the last vial. Instead of pouring in one nanometer of pyro-oil, she used only a half nanometer.

The last vial changed color from the dim yellow to a fluorescent yellow.

It did not disintegrate.

The room was completely silent for a minute.

"You've done it!" shouted Ray, clasping her on the back and almost causing Mia to drop more of the pyro-gel into the last vial.

The three assistants crowded around the glove box, peering in.

A commanding voice rose through the hubbub of excitement. "Before we claim victory, let's administer it to the specimen." The Chief walked over to stand beside Mia and nodded at the huge red Naga that coiled itself inside the next room.

"Okay," said Mia. Her hands still in the glove box, she poured her mixture into a small receptacle. The receptacle hissed shut. A cylindrical pipe went from the glove box through the piping in the floor and up the wall and ended up at an ejector nozzle in the room the Naga was in.

Mia pulled out her hands from the micro-gravity science glove box and shook them free. She went to her computer that stood several feet away from the glove box. The keyboard made too loud a noise as she typed in the command: EXECUTE. She hit 'Enter.'

The red Naga in the other room rose up suddenly. As if it could sense the biological weapon being released.

The lights in the entire lab beeped and a red sign activated: BIOLOGICAL

CONTAINMENT RELEASED. A siren sounded. Mia cursed herself for forgetting to turn off the lab failsafe.

But it didn't matter.

The biological weapon now entered the Naga's room and dispersed in a bright yellow jet right in front of the snake. The Naga shot up suddenly. Its blue eyes widened. Its face showed a shocked expression. It hissed again, its hood flaring, and reared its head and spat. A viscous fluid slammed into the remaining glass and evaporated. More alarms began to blare.

The Naga's head slammed through the glass. Its face turned a dark blue; its forked tongue engorged; its scales shredded against the edge of the glass. The Naga's body jolted and shuddered. Its mouth opened and screamed, "Nooo!" And then its head slumped to the ground, dead.

Mia shook all over. Evelyn stood there, her feet wide apart, holding up a gun.

"It worked," she said.

The lab's failsafe kicked in and the air-cleansers took out any remaining contaminants in the air. The alarms finally went away.

"It worked," said Mia. All she could remember was the human-like scream the Naga made as the biological weapon destroyed it from inside out.

"What are you going to name it?" asked Evelyn.

Mia started. "Name what?"

"It is customary for the inventor to name the invention, or for the invention to be named after the inventor. You've just invented a biological weapon that will work against the Nagaplex. Well done."

"I don't know," said Mia.

"Agent Yellow," said Ray, her boss. "We can call it Agent Yellow."

Chapter 26

Paarty

Rest & Recuperation Day
Yalata Township
26 February 2076
19:30

The township of Yalata stood in the middle of nowhere. A town that made money from the miners who lived there during their two-week shift and from the Earth Defense Force soldiers visiting during their R&R—Rest and Recuperation. Those visits had dwindled in the last ten years and the mining had dried up, leaving behind the husk of a town.

The bouncing Wild-Boar jeep sat six soldiers. The entire Alpha One Tango squad: Ben, Jadyn, Natalie, and Zhi, and their two honorary members from two other squads: Matt and Andy.

"Yeah, everyone's gonna be there," said Andy. "Imagine all those hot girls from the Air Force."

"And the fishes from the Navy," said Matt.

Ben laughed. He was nervous. His ex-girlfriend, Julie, might be there. He wondered if she was still with Keith McAllister.

Zhi shook her head and rolled her eyes. "Behave."

"It's the only Rest and Recuperation day we're going to get," said Natalie. "Try not to spoil it or get in trouble." She pointedly did not look at Jadyn.

Everyone had been tiptoeing around Jadyn since his complete meltdown. When he told them about his younger brother Denzel it all made sense.

They reached Yalata and went through the center of town, which consisted of a wide road edged with tufts of grass and sand. The Jeep entered a huge tunnel with large crossbeams. The tunnel ended at a massive roundabout in the middle of the town that spun off into four streets.

Ten helipads stretched over the top of the tunnel. Usually each spot was empty. Today every helipad sat occupied by a bristling G15-Venator, the attack helicopters used by the Air Force that were named after the apex dinosaur Afrovenator.

As they parked the Jeep, Ben thought Yalata looked like a corpse dressed in Christmas lights. Many other Wild-Boars slotted themselves into the vertical parking lot in a marked off section in the middle of the road.

Fast food restaurants, pubs, and a corner gas station edged the road. A bullet-riddled sign that said 'Fuel Your Soul at Yalata' rotated over the gas station.

"Wow, I haven't seen anyone else from a different military division since I came to base," said Ben, pointing at all the Navy and Air Force vehicles. Each major division within the Earth Defense Force had different license plates.

"Where should we go?" asked Natalie. "I think we should find a nice bar. Something with a pool table and good food."

"Now that is a girl right after my own heart," said Andy, a big goofy grin splitting his face.

Natalie blushed. She tucked an errant bit of wispy red hair behind her ear. Except her head was shaved. Like everyone else. It made her blush even more.

"How about we walk around?" said Ben. He secretly didn't want to get into a bar where there were Air Force personnel.

"Sounds good," said Zhi. "Lead on."

"Do you think it's the last time we'll get to spend socially?" asked Natalie.

"Nah, we'll party a lot after we kill those snakes. They don't call me Mister Mongoose for nothing," said Andy.

Everyone laughed. Jadyn kept quiet. He'd been quiet ever since his mental explosion. Ben missed the loud, boisterous Jadyn. He wanted that Jadyn back.

They walked around Yalata. When they met a group of other grunts they talked to them. Though, they were a bit more wary around the other groups of Navy and Air Force rats.

"Why are they all so small?" Jadyn asked suddenly. He'd been quiet the entire night.

"Everyone is small compared to you," said Ben.

Zhi gave Ben a look and shook her head. "Air Force and navy don't take the growth hormones."

"Really?" Natalie said.

"Well, I guess it makes sense as they won't be fighting them on the ground like we will be," said Matt.

"They do take the learner accelerators, though," said Zhi.

"Let's not talk about it," said Ben. "I just want to forget about all that."

"Guys, let's check out this cool bar. It's on the edge of town. Shouldn't be many people there," said Andy. "I checked it on my phone."

Alpha One Tango made a rule that nobody would use their phones while they were in Yalata partying. It was the first time they'd gotten their phones back after handing them over on day one. It was also the first time they got to wear civilian clothes.

A lot of the recruits were using their phones, talking to their friends and family as they walked about town. There had been strict no outside comms rules enforced on base. Ben wasn't ready to give his guardian a call yet.

The squad walked around a bend and noticed the heavy presence of MPs— military police—dressed in their military fatigues with the blue berets.

They had walked a fair distance away from the center of town. The bar, Bat-sh!t Crazy, lay in a quiet corner of Yalata with only two cars parked out front. No sign of Wild-Boar Jeeps and it was too far away from the G15-Venators for any Air Force brats to bother with.

Country music came from within. Ben pulled open the door and held it. "Go ahead, guys." Andy, Natalie, Matt, Zhi, and Jadyn strode in.

Jadyn had to duck his head to avoid banging it against the top of the doorframe.

The inside consisted of a high ceiling with two balconies that looked down. The walls were made of slats of polished wood. The music wasn't too loud. The place was clean. Folk stood on those balconies eating and drinking. Two pool tables occupied either end of the ground floor. A bar stood against the wall lit by a yellow backlight. The bottles of spirits glowed. A huge bartender wearing a muggy apron wiped down one end of the bar. He eyed the newcomers and nodded.

Ben, feeling euphoric, said, "Emu Export please. Six large glasses. Drinks on me!"

"Ooorah!" the squad cheered.

The bartender clunked six huge mugs down on the table. He nodded and shoved them a bowl with a packet of potato chips. "On the house."

"Gee, thanks," said Ben.

"Here's to the best squad in the EDF," said Jadyn, holding out his beer mug.

"Best squad in the EDF," said Andy.

"Best squad," said Zhi.

"I wonder if General Katana drinks beer," said Ben, after clinking his beer mug. Some of the foamy beer slopped onto his wrist. The Emu Export left a crisp tang in his mouth.

They all took their initial swallows. Natalie grimaced. She tapped her chest. "Wow, it's strong."

Andy patted her back as she coughed. "Easy sips do it."

Jadyn laughed. "This ain't strong, sister. Just wait till we hit the spirits."

Ben felt good to be with his squad. Three months ago had come and gone. He couldn't even remember the kid he used to be.

"I can't believe this is our vacation day before the mission. Anyone going to call home?" Ben asked.

"Done and dusted," said Andy.

Jadyn shrugged. Natalie looked down. Those two were a definite no.

"I called Mom," said Matt. "Bored me to tears talking about her cat."

"I should call Annie," said Ben. "Mia's mom. She was the one who took me in after the Nagas killed Dad."

"Yeah you should," said Zhi.

That was the end of the serious conversation. Soon it turned into like it was back in high school. Matt and Andy were such goons and made everyone laugh.

For a couple hours they talked complete crap. There were many questions about what General Katana wore to bed. Ben said full samurai armor and Andy spat out half his beer. Matt did an impression of General Katana that had everyone in stitches. The six soldiers enjoyed warmth of the bar and let the nice alcohol fuzz creep over them.

"Guys, let's play some pool," said Natalie.

They stumbled toward the closest pool table. An Air Force couple occupied it. Ben could tell just by the superior way they held themselves. And there was something familiar about the man.

The man chalked his cue stick. "You Army rats are a loud bunch," he said.

For a moment Ben thought he'd misheard.

"What the heck did you just say?" said Jadyn, stepping up to him. He towered over the guy. But they must have bred arrogance to a whole new level because he didn't even have the common sense to back up a step.

"Play for the table?" asked Andy, inserting himself between Jadyn and the guy. He casually draped his hand against a corner.

"No," said the man, eyeing Jadyn. Something about his swagger told Ben he was an F33-Boomerang jet fighter jock. His girlfriend was beautiful too.

"You can have the table," said the girl. Blonde hair spilled out of her blue cap. She reached for him but he pulled away.

"No, these mud suckers aren't wanted in here," said the man.

"You got a problem?" Jadyn slammed his beer mug down in the middle of the pool table.

"No we don't," said the girl. She obviously hadn't drunk as much as the guy. "Keith, let's just go. Now."

"These dregs of humanity," said the boy. His breath stank of Emu Export. He pushed Jadyn.

Ben quickly slipped between Jadyn and the boy. "Hey, hold it."

Something familiar about the boy pulled at Ben. Ben's eyes widened in recognition just as the boy's eyes widened in shock.

"Keith McAllister?"

"Ben Williams?"

The girl who stood next to the boy dropped her beer. The sour smell of beer filled the air. "Ben?" she squeaked. The hardened glass bounced and stopped at Ben's feet. Beer and foam drenched his boots. But all he could do was stare.

"Julie?" he said. It had been three months since he'd seen his ex-girlfriend. The loss of her slammed him right in the solar plexus.

Her blond hair, which had once gone down to her back, now curtained her jawline. If anything it highlighted the beauty of her face. The F33-Boomerang badge sat on the left collar of her civilian t-shirt. Tanned arms and legs peeked out from a blue dress. She wore blue high heels. Ben was about to congratulate her on making it into the F33 fighter program when a shriek had him reaching for his weapon. A weapon that he did not carry.

"You!" screeched Keith McAllister. His right eye looked much bluer than his left eye. That was what gave it away. It was an implant. And he'd needed that implant because Ben had ripped his eyeball out of its socket only three months ago.

"Get away from her!" shrieked Keith.

Ben flinched. Realizing he'd reached for Julie's hand to shake it. Keith interposed and pushed Ben back. He wouldn't have fallen, but he slipped on spilt beer, grabbed for the pool cue—its thin shaft of wood leaned itself against the table. It snapped under the force of his grab and he slammed his head against the side of the table and then he only saw the horizontal view of the bar. For some reason people were standing upside down.

"You Army bug. I can't wait until you're Naga meat. How long do you think you'll last, Ben? You know what the average lifespan for an Army grunt dropped into a hot LZ is?" Keith's face twisted in rage over him. "You're all going to frigging die. Julie and I will be safe in our boomerangs raining hellfire on the Nagaplex."

A burst of pain radiated from between Ben's legs. Keith's boots stomped into his groin. Ben curled into a fetal position as the pain screamed into his belly.

Keith aimed a kick at Jadyn's groin and hit his huge knee instead.

Jadyn howled and thundered into Keith. Julie screamed and jumped on Jadyn's back.

Dozens of other Air Force soldiers came from above. More came from the other pool table. "Oh shizz!" Andy said. "There's fifteen of them blues. We walked into an Air Force pub."

An Air Force soldier slammed a fist into Jadyn's ribs. The big kid groaned. Several other Air Force soldiers converged on Jadyn. They clung to him like ants over a giant but he did not go down.

Meanwhile an Air Force pilot, judging by the G15-Venator badge on her collar, kicked out at Natalie. Natalie ducked and hauled Ben to his feet and in that same movement she backhanded the Air Force pilot right in the head. The force of her hit sent the other woman collapsing to the ground. Knocked out cold.

Jadyn roared. Fifteen Air Force brats clung on to him. They looked like blue ants. He turned in a circle and roared. The brats flew into the air, bouncing against the walls. One slammed into the pool table and one went over the bar and smashed into the Johnny Walkers filling the air with malt and vanilla.

A distant siren filled the background.

Ben ducked as a pool stick came for his head. The stick whooshed over his head and would've taken out his eye. He growled but Andy and Matt tackled the Air Force brat to the ground and choked him out.

A loud boom came from outside. As Ben's back was to the pub's entrance, he didn't see the military police swinging their electrical batons.

The world winked out of existence.

ૡ

"You've got to be frigging joking me!" shouted James Roberts, Marshall General of the military police, as he stood staring out from his desk at the soldiers standing at attention in front of him.

The General of the Air Force, Ben Harper, stood stiffer than a plank right next to him. The General of the Army, Katana Bugeisha, stood to his left. They radiated displeasure.

"How do eighty Air Force and Army brats get into a spat in a bar licensed to hold only forty of you?!" roared James

Roberts. "You should all be bloody whipped until your backs are ribboned." He looked like he was in an apoplectic fit. His jowls quivered and his faced reddened more than a tomato.

Ben and his squad formed a line with all the other fifteen kids from the Air Force. Every kid who'd started the altercation stood in this room wishing they hadn't been a part of it.

For a moment Ben closed his eyes. He'd been tasered by the military police and his body still hurt everywhere. He squeezed his eyes shut and re-opened them. Julie stood to the right of him with the rest of her Air Force buddies. He couldn't help but turn to look at her.

"Something distracting you, soldier?" whipped out the Chief's voice.

"No, sir," Ben replied.

The Marshall General strode to the front of them and dumped the huge life-sized cardboard poster of Imperator Kaali in front of them. The huge Naga towered over twenty feet high and wider than three soldiers. "That's the frigging enemy!" he shouted.

"Sir, the fault is mine. I take full responsibility," said Zhi, stepping forward.

"No, sir, it's my fault," said Jadyn, stepping forward with a salute. "I acted with violence."

"Sir, I'm to blame," said Natalie. "I didn't try to stop my team." She stepped forward too.

"Sir, me and the Air Force brat had beef between us. It's really me who should shoulder this blame," said Ben, joining them.

None of the Air Force brats stepped forward.

"You would ordinarily be court-martialed," said the Marshall General. "But in five days' time we engage in our last desperate battle with the Nagas. It's do or die."

General Katana walked in front of the group. She walked right to left, staring at Ben, Natalie, Jadyn, and finally her eyes settled on Zhi. It was Zhi who bore the brunt of that gaze.

General Katana said, "It was an Air Force pilot who sacrificed his life to get me to the Nagaplex. And it was an Army brat who managed to infiltrate the Nagas and find out about the hatcheries. It was a Navy brat who managed to save the Army brat and bring her back to this base. We are one team. I'm disappointed in you, Squad Leader Zhi. You have let down the Earth Defense Force."

Ben felt like Zhi was bearing the worst of the scolding. That wasn't fair. General Katana was the most famous hero in the Earth Defense Force. She was the face of the war. Her posters plastered themselves everywhere in New York.

"I'm sorry," Zhi said, looking down.

Ben had never seen Zhi so deflated.

Chapter 27

The Bugeishas

Ten Years Ago…

Japan, Okinawa
3 January 2067
07:30

"Harder," shouted Onna Bugeisha, as she stared down at her six-year-old sister, Zhi Bugeisha.

Zhi's lower lip trembled. Her dark hair plastered itself with sweat over her forehead. Tears smeared her eyebrows and snot oozed her nose.

If there hadn't been blood on the six-year-old's knuckles she would've made an adorable picture. Moms and dads would've picked up the child and showered her with kisses.

Zhi wore a plain karate gi unadorned with any patches or symbols. She sported a frayed old white belt around her hips. The uniform looked too big for such a small child.

The two Bugeishas stood in the old family dojo that had been handed down through the Bugeisha bloodline for the last one thousand five hundred years. The Bugeishas traced their heritage all the way back to the Edo period.

The Japanese red pine flooring covered itself with sweat and blood. The hot heat from the noonday sun blared ahead, making it like a steam room inside. The smell of warm wood and sweat filled the dojo.

Six-year-old Zhi stood in front of a makiwara—a thick wooden post with handles that jutted out to the sides.

"Full force. Hajime!" commanded Onna. "Ichi!"

Zhi shouted, "Kiai!" each time Onna sensei counted. She punched from her hips, her small fists smacking into the surface of the makiwara and making thudding noises.

At the sixth count Zhi flinched as the pain ripped through her knuckles. Her knuckles, already bleeding, tore to show the first sign of the white bone underneath.

"What are you stopping for? Do you think a Naga will stop as it chokes you to death with its tail? Each time you stop we shall begin again. From the start. Full force. Hajime!"

Zhi closed her eyes as she reached out to punch. The pain ricocheted through her fists, into her knuckles, where it screamed like a thousand ghouls in Zhi's brain. It felt like the time she'd burned her hand over the stove, except this felt sharper.

"Yame!" Sensei Onna shouted at her student to stop. She stood at the edge of the dojo and bowed before entering the center. Honoring the spirit of her samurai ancestors who stared at her from ancient pictures on the wall.

Zhi flinched like she'd been slapped.

"You are finished for the day. You do not deserve the honor of punching this makiwara post with such pitiful effort. Go and meditate."

Zhi bowed. Her hands shook as she clasped them by her side. She backed away from her sensei, ensuring she faced her sensei as she did so. To turn her back would be dishonorable.

Onna Bugeisha sported a white gi with a frayed black belt. She stood in front of the makiwara in ready posture. In a sudden burst of movement and with a shout of "Kiai!" she began punching the makiwara.

Each hit reverberated the entire maki-wara. The chi energy from Onna's punches vibrated the floor and made the tatami mats jump. The punches carried so much energy.

Onna kept punching even after her knuckles cracked. She kept punching even when the bone marrow oozed out from the split cartilage of her knuckles. She didn't flinch. She didn't pause. Not once.

Onna counted her punches from ten to one thousand. And then to ten thousand. The hot sun baked the dojo. Eventually, Onna collapsed to her knees. She didn't stop punching. She kept punching. Each punch with the full force of her chi. Eventually after twelve hours when her hands looked like mangled stumps, the heat and exhaustion took its toll and she collapsed.

Zhi, who had been sitting cross-legged on the tatami mats that lined the edge of the dojo, stood up and ran to her sister. She held a bottle of water in her hand. She knelt down and lifted her sister's dazed face up. Fine salt crusted Onna's cheeks as Zhi poured water through cracked lips.

Zhi called to the small nurse robot that stood to the side of the dojo, silent until now. The nurse-bot slid forward on two smooth tires.

Zhi grunted as she went to Onna's back and pushed. She wrapped her little hands around her sister and held out Onna's dangling limb. She pointed to the bleeding stumps that had once been her sister's hands. The nurse robot warbled something and then a nozzle came out of its chassis. A thick gel substance spread itself over Onna's left and right hands.

ॐ

The very next morning Zhi faced the makiwara post. Her face set, her jaws taut with determination.

Her knuckles still bruised. The whites still visible.

Zhi took a deep breath.

"Kiai!" she screamed and slammed her fists against the makiwara post. The pain screamed at her. She ignored it. She kept punching until the whites oozed out of her knuckles. She kept at it until eventually she tired and fainted.

Zhi trained like that from the age of five until seventeen. No friends. No birthdays. Just the rage of her ancestors powering her on.

And on her seventeenth birthday she joined the Earth Defense Force. To her surprise, she discovered the soldiers didn't call her sister by her given name, Onna. They called her Katana.

General Katana.

Chapter 28

Ambushed!

Mia swallowed as the shuttle cut through the clouds and entered the air space of the Earth Defense Force. Two space marines from the Planetfall Troopers division sat across from her, and the Chief Admiral sat next to her. It was Mia's first visit to Australia and she came with weapons. That didn't feel right.

The Earth military base looked like a guard who was too old and didn't know it, and still wanted to serve in the military. It was a throwback to the glory days of the Earth Defense Force. The huge buildings were old and rust-worn. The majority of them looked dark; only a few held lights, and those concentrated themselves in the middle of the base.

"The majority of men and women who served were wiped out during Operation Python," Chief Admiral Evelyn Wilson said in a quiet voice. "We've been diverting resources to the SDF for quite a while now. We assumed Earth would be overrun by the Nagas. And that a space presence would save the human race."

Mia was shocked. She'd spend her entire school life in a military curriculum and she'd never been told the truth.

"This is really a last attempt by the Earth's military and General Katana. The SDF has come to the table and delivered them the bomb. It's really up to them now." The Chief pursed her lips as the sky outside darkened.

"A lot of my friends had family who died in Operation Python," said Mia. She remembered the announcement of Operation Python back when she started high school. General Katana was one of a handful of survivors. Julie's father died. He'd been a fighter pilot. Now Julie followed in his footsteps.

The pilotless shuttle banked suddenly. Below them the huge landing zone of Capital Base Oceania stared back at them. Yellow lights dotted the runway. A soldier holding glowing batons signaled to them.

Mia turned in her seat and looked back at the rear of the shuttle. The huge pellet had the ominous mark of the black skull on the yellow background. The word 'Biohazard' was stamped in red just below it.

"Katana's going to be angry. The intelligence we received is very late," said Evelyn. "And we've brought only a single crate of Agent Yellow." She grunted as the seatbelts fastened themselves around them.

"Prepare for landing," boomed the autopilot's voice.

༄

The door swung open and two space marines stepped inside the administrative office. They saluted crisply as they stepped to the side. Chief Admiral Evelyn Wilson strode into view from between them.

General Katana, General Harper, and Marshall General Roberts turned around with astonishment on their faces.

"Generals, this base is under imminent attack. Nagas. You need to deploy soon," said the Chief Admiral. "This is Special Project Lead Scientist Mia Johnson-Patel. She is the creator of Agent Yellow. The biological agent is ready to deploy and use against the Nagaplex. We have loaded it into one of the G15-Venators."

Ben couldn't believe it. Mia was right in front of his eyes. But that thought was wiped out when he registered what the Chief Admiral just said.

General Katana went to her desk. She pressed a red button and the sound of static and crackling filtered through. "Defcon 1. This is General Katana. Operation King Cobra is now live. Deploy. Deploy. Defcon 1." She typed on the old and battered keyboard in front of a black screen with green fonts. "I've alerted all the other three capital bases."

Now that's how a general acts, thought Ben. No questions, no ifs or buts, just straight to action.

Sirens wailed in the night and filtered into the General's office.

For a split second all the generals stared at each other.

"General Harper, I need a pilot," said General Katana.

"You have two. Airwoman Harrington and Airman McAllister, report to General Katana for duty."

Julie and Keith saluted at their general. Julie said, "Sir, my pilot specialization was not in the G15s."

"Adapt. Learn. There's a reason that's the Air Force motto." He patted Julie and Keith on the back. "You're my best two." Then he bolted out of the room with the remaining Air Force soldiers following behind him.

"I'm going to get the base defenses sorted. Good luck and Godspeed," said Marshall General Roberts. The salute he gave General Katana held a finality to it. He sprinted out of the room.

276

"Follow me," said General Katana. "The Black Berets need to be deployed first. They are our best hope."

𝄞

Outside the base was chaos.

Ben wanted desperately to grab Mia and ask her about the biological agent. What was that all about? Before leaving the General's room, they pilfered the rifle cabinet. They held their M18s as they jogged out. Zhi took point. No words were spoken; they went into formation seamlessly.

"Katana, I don't think you have time to get the Black Berets," said the Chief Admiral.

General Katana's office was in the administrative wing of the capital base. "That's where we're heading to right now. They have an assembly point."

Ben's world appeared through the sights on his M18. A calm descended over him. I've done this before, he realized. Many times.

The dark night flared with the flash of red from the siren on top of the administrative building. Ben's senses went into overload. It was like he developed a sixth sense. Every shadow analyzed and discarded. He was conscious of the fact they didn't have any armor on.

The barracks of the Black Berets stood across from the administrative area, separated by a wide road used by tanks. The barracks resembled small, brightly lit individual apartments. They were the most lethal and effective group in the history of Earth Defense Force infantry. Only fifty of them remained.

General Katana and Alpha One Tango strode across the road. A rumbling sensation went through the ground and right up to the soles of their feet.

It was a very unsettling sensation when the entire world twisted on its axis. Ben felt there wasn't anything he could control. His first thought was of protecting Mia.

The Black Berets stood armed and fully assembled just outside their barracks. They immediately ran toward General Katana shouting at her and waving their hands.

Ben couldn't hear them through the roar of the sirens, jets taking off, and the earthquake rumbling beneath his feet. Why were the Black Berets waving at them?

"Back!" yelled General Katana. She turned on her robotic feet, her torso swiveling around, and she bolted back the way they' just come.

The earth heaved and buckled beneath them. It happened so fast they didn't even have time to go back.

The ground erupted in front of them right beneath the running Black Berets. The force threw the Black Berets into the air like globs of earth. One of them landed with a thump at Ben's feet, his neck skewed at an odd angle.

A monstrous, gigantic worm burst out from the earth. A roar so loud glass shattered from the sound waves that followed. The creature kept rising and rising, until it was almost as tall and wide as the World Trade Center.

The monster's mouth was wider than the doors of largest hangars on base. Long tentacles covered its back and lashed at the air. One of the tentacles grabbed a

Black Beret. The thick, ropy strands of muscles squeezed him so hard his body looked about to pop. He turned to sludge as bright green acid oozed from the tentacle. His scream died as his esophagus melted into his ribcage.

All the bodies of Black Berets lay dead. Most twisted at odd angles. The most elite fighting force in Earth Defense Force history wiped out in seconds.

The giant worm slammed into the ground, causing a rippling wave of force that flared out throughout the entire base.

Ben knew death when he saw it. There was nothing he could do to avert it right then.

The gigantic worm whipped its head up as an F33-Boomerang flew into the air and peppered it with missiles. Chunks of flesh showered into the air. The worm was too heavy and large to snatch at the F33s. It roared and headed straight toward the middle of the base where the C10-M Super Titans were being prepped.

"Which hangar did you arrive in?" asked General Katana, her eyes darted to the woman on the ground.

Mia huddled on the ground with the pain grimacing face of Chief Admiral Evelyn Wilson in her lap. The chief's breathing frothed with blood. A piece of shrapnel had cut through her ribcage and soaked through her entire purple uniform.

Mia's face was streaked with tears. Her hands shook as she cradled the Chief's head.

"Which hangar?" General Katana asked again, this time to Evelyn.

Mia looked up, her face pale and shocked.

"Hangar one hundred eight," said Chief Admiral Evelyn Wilson.

"Lyn, thank you. You came just in time," said General Katana, leaning down and holding the Chief's hand.

"Who are you taking now that you don't have the berets?" the Chief asked.

General Katana beckoned at the squad members of Alpha One Tango.

"They're just kids. You needed the Black Berets."

"They're soldiers now. They'll have to do."

"Always improvising…" Those were the last words from Chief Admiral Evelyn

Wilson's mouth before she fainted. The bright blood looked like strawberry jam on her pale face.

General Katana ripped out the shrapnel from Evelyn's ribcage that caused the admiral to heave and her eyelids fluttered. Katana tore slivers of the Chief's uniform and wound a makeshift tourniquet around the wound. She grabbed a vial from her military webbing and jabbed the Chief with adrenaline, and the Chief opened her eyes and sucked in a gasp of air again.

General Katana said, "Head to the medics. I... We need you to survive."

"Take Mia. You'll need her," stammered the Chief.

"Let's go! Go! Go!" General Katana shouted at the rest of them.

Ben grabbed at Mia and hauled her up. "Get it together, soldier!" He unstrapped his handgun, a H5 Boxer, and shoved it into her shaking hands. "Shoot baddies." He wasn't sure if it was a good idea giving her the gun. She hadn't had the same set of training, but it seemed better than nothing. "Follow behind me."

General Katana sprinted toward a lone bus that somehow hadn't been too damaged. It had a front right flat tire slit by shrapnel, judging by all the crap surrounding it. "Get in!" the General shouted at them as she squashed herself into the driver's seat.

Julie, Keith, Mia, and all the squad members of Alpha One Tango and Andy and Matt piled into the bus. Zhi was the last one in, her rifle held out providing cover for the others.

"It's the last hangar," said General Katana. "A good choice. Safe." The bus thundered to life and the General floored it. "We could have had a few minutes earlier warning."

Ben sat next to Mia. She kept shivering. He held her hand. "It's okay. We'll get out of this."

Julie and Keith exchanged stares. They looked shaken. Blood smeared itself across Julie's forehead.

Zhi held her assault rifle, a grim determination across her face. She took the front of the bus. Jadyn took the rear of the bus, holding out his gun. And Natalie was in the middle, staring out left and right as they zoomed past burning buildings going up in flames. Matt and Andy stayed up at the front near the General.

The huge monstrous worm left a trail of destruction in its wake. It also left a wide pathway like it was some type of bulldozer. The bus jumped and bucked as it went over bits of rocks, crates, and dead bodies.

None of Alpha One Tango lost their cool. This was what their training had been for. Ben knew Zhi would feel insulted that the chief had called them kids. Zhi had been training her entire life for this. She didn't know anything else. This was the purpose of her existence. Zhi was born a Black Beret.

༃

The C10-M Super Titans roared as their engines prepped for takeoff. Within ten minutes of General Katana sending out the defcon alert and giving the orders for Operation King Cobra to be executed, all twenty pilots had rushed toward the giant twenty-mile circle that was the tarmac where the twenty C10-Ms parked themselves. Each could hold five thousand troops.

Now the pilots worked with ground control to fill every single C10-M as soon as humanly possible with a hundred thousand soldiers rushing toward the tarmac.

Ben stared through the windows on the bus as General Katana sped across the runway. Outside the C10M Super Titans looked like huge round-shaped UFOs sitting on the ground. Already the refueling pipes snaked into their bellies, pumping vigorously. Ground crews strode around like ants.

A hundred thousand soldiers converged on the C10-Ms. The trundling troop transport towers were crammed full of soldiers. Soldiers ran on the tarmac, avoiding bustling vehicles and weapon crates being loaded and unloaded.

It was pure chaos.

And the giant monstrous worm headed right into the middle of that chaos of jet fuel, transport towers, and hot engine C10Ms getting ready for takeoff.

More busses, Jeeps, and even motorcycles filled with soldiers headed toward the

C10Ms. Several platoons came running out of a warehouse on foot.

F33-Boomerangs filled the air with their shrill whine as they cut through the air and peppered the worm to prevent it from getting to the C10Ms.

The worm reared into the air. Thousands of legs twittered, looking like the underbelly of a cockroach. As massive as the C10Ms were the worm dwarfed them. A huge disgusting slit looking like a bum hole opened up where its face should've been. A green poisonous liquid splashed out.

Explosions rocked the fuel supply tanks that were stored underground. Bits of road and fuel flared into the air. Several of the C10Ms' fuselages exploded in a fiery hailstorm.

Two C10Ms rose into the air vertically, leaving troops dangling from their hatches as they hastened to take off before the worm could get to them. The worm launched its body into the air, bringing down both C10Ms. The worm and the C10Ms slammed into the earth, causing a rippling, cascading chain reaction as every single underground fuel tank exploded in turn. The stored munitions in the adjoining warehouses went up in flames.

An F33-Boomerang whizzed past the roaring and flailing worm that was now burning alive. The worm stretched into the air, trying to get away from the roaring flames, and the F33 dove right into its throat, sending out a splash of viscous liquid, organs, and green acid that ate the fighter jet instantly.

The worm slammed to the ground, sending out a force like a nuclear detonation.

General Katana had just managed to get the bus to the last hangar on the tarmac when the force from the falling worm flipped the bus and rotated it into the air. The bus flew like a spear, smashing through the closed doors of hangar number one hundred eight.

꒰

Ben groaned as the world bent and straightened, and bent and straightened in front of him repeatedly. The bus lay on its side and the smell of burning gas and rubber shoved itself into Ben's nose. Mia lay against a cracked window with a massively bleeding forehead. He quickly felt for her pulse. Sighing in relief, he picked her up.

"To me," shouted Jadyn. He used his immense strength and battered the front windscreen. The windscreen wipers melted like stringy licorice on the ground almost tripped him.

General Katana wasn't anywhere to be found.

Zhi helped Mat and Andy out of the bus, as they'd been badly bruised.

Keith McAllister's body had impaled itself through one of the steel poles that connected the end of the seats to the roof of the bus.

"Natalie, you okay?" Ben asked as he kicked away a burning, stinking tyre that lay on Natalie's leg. Her body twisted itself in a pretzel pose underneath a seat.

Somehow, she managed to twist herself out from under the seat. She still held her M18 in her hand. A smile sat on her face streaked with smoke. "Alpha One

Tango, good to go." A hysterical laugh came from her throat.

Together they struggled out of the bus.

"Status?" asked Zhi. Not a single emotion except determination etched itself on her face. Strength radiated from her and Ben drew it in.

Ben looked around worried. Where was Julie?

Natalie had a hurt left leg. Jadyn had suffered a shoulder gash that showed bone. That would need attending. Ben had a mild burn on his right palm.

"There." Zhi pointed.

General Katana stood below the rear ramp of the G15-Venator talking to Julie. The younger girl kept nodding. Shell-shocked. The General put a hand on her shoulder and looked into her eyes. That contact brought more life into Julie.

"The coordinates are already loaded. I need you to fly behind the enemy lines and drop. We are going to the Naga-plex. I know you've specialized in flying F33-Boomerangs. But think about it this way—the Venator has thicker armor, better firepower." The General didn't point out the weaknesses of the fact the Venator was like piloting a slug in comparison to a F33. Or that it required a lot more coordination since it was normally flown by two pilots. They were down to one.

Julie laughed. Her voice held a tinge of hysteria.

"You've got this," said General Katana.

Ben chimed in. "Jules, you've been dreaming about this since you were a kid, right? Time to make your uncle and dad proud."

Julie looked at him and nodded, swallowing hard.

Chapter 29

Six o'clock

The G15-Venator's quadcopter blades sent vibrations through the six occupied seats and right into Ben's jaw. His teeth rattled with adrenaline, nerves, and fear as they flew over Capital Base Oceania. His fingers pressed against the cold metal ledge of the round window.

There was a big black crater where there used to be the middle of the major runway. The destruction was so big and grave that a sense of complete black hopelessness made Ben feel as if he'd choked on a bone.

"Ben, I need to speak with you," said a voice. It whispered insistently by his side. His irises reflected the blooming orange explosions that continued to rocket through the base. How many weapons did the Earth Defense Force stockpile in that exact area? The Nagas targeted their enemies with extreme prejudice. In one fell swoop they'd made Operation King Cobra extinct.

Soft lips touched his. Ben blinked as Mia's face blurred into focus. Confusion reigned. Where was he again?

"Ben, we need to talk," said Mia. "Over there."

The G15 held twenty seats and most of them stood empty. Alpha One Tango occupied the front row, and Andy and Matt took two seats in the second.

Ben followed Mia to the rear of the quadcopter and slumped to the ground. General Katana's voice came from the cockpit. She was talking to Central Command. He could tell by the brief discernible words things were not good.

"Ben," Mia said.

Ben shook himself and straightened up. "Sorry, what's up?"

Jadyn's huge form tapped Mia on the shoulder. She turned and looked up at him in surprise. "I'm sorry for what I did to you back on Family Day. I was an idiot." He saluted and went back to sit next to Natalie.

Mia looked confused.

"You don't recognize Jadyn, do you?" Ben asked.

"Jadyn?" she said. "Really? He's huge."

Ben nodded. "And that was Natalie."

"That's Natalie?" Mia's eyes widened in shock. "She looks so different. She's buff. I mean he's buff too. You all are."

Ben laughed and wrapped his hands around his childhood friend in a quick hug. "We'll get out of this. Trust me, Mia." Had she kissed him? He couldn't even remember. But she stiffened underneath his embrace.

"Listen, we don't have much time," she said. Her dark brown eyes darted left and right.

Mia's walnut-brown skin appeared weathered. Her wide-spaced eyes narrowed with fatigue. Where Ben remembered her mouth in a constant smile revealing her ever-present tooth gap, now her lips pressed tight. She wore augmented glasses that displayed an assortment of ever shifting data. When their eyes touched hers always slid away.

"What is it?" He held her clammy hands like he did when they were children.

She looked down at his grasp and gently disentangled herself.

"Did the SDF treat you right?" he asked.

She laughed. It held a tinge of hysteria.

"Ben, the Agent Yellow. It's not safe. When it gets deployed ensure you are very far away—"

Footsteps clanked behind them as General Katana emerged from the cockpit. Immediately, they all made to stand but she waved them down. "Sit, it's going to be a rough ride. I've got these talons for feet and they can hold on to anything."

An old and battered display panel hung on the wall next to the cockpit. She turned the knob to 'On' and the black and green display flared to life.

ᘒ

/ EDF Priority Broadcast

Nagas have attacked all four Capital Bases, killing a total of three hundred sixty thousand soldiers. Approximately ten thousand soldiers have escaped from each base. Most of them aboard smaller transport vessels.

The Nagas' ambush displayed an uncanny precision and timing, the Nagas targeted high traffic density areas just as our soldiers boarded the C10M Super-Titans.

The intelligence from SDF's Strategic Space Command allowed us to save soldier lives, even though it came much too late.

General Katana has called Operation King Cobra forward. All forces, immediately head to Nagaplex rendezvous. Follow General Katana's battle plan.

Operation King Cobra is green to go. God be with you.

/ End

"Special Projects Lead Scientist, give us instructions on how to deploy the Agent Yellow," ordered General Katana.

Ben gave Mia a thumb's up of encouragement as she stood up and went to stand beside the display.

Mia said, "Agent Yellow is a bioweapon made after discovering that the Nagaplex is alive. We at the SDF hypothesize it's a giant-sized Naga. We have tested Agent Yellow in our labs." She swallowed and wiped the sweat from her brow. She stammered a lot when she spoke.

"Are these the weapons?" Ben asked.

At the rear of the quadcopter, red netting cascaded down around the cargo bay. A blue casket capsule stood with biohazard stickers at each corner. Mia walked to the back. Jadyn ripped apart the netting and stuffed it into one of the side cabinets.

Mia put her palm against the side of the casket and it hissed open. Fog rolled out of it onto the floor, obscuring the yellow-striped lines. Six rectangular panels sat inside the casket with handles sticking out.

Mia reached for one of those handles and pulled out something that looked like a kettlebell. Except these had a digital reading on the side of them. "This is how to arm them," she said. She twisted the handle to three o'clock. "When you hit six o'clock it will be active. You cannot turn these back once you hit six o'clock. The three o'clock position can be used to set it into the target." As she twisted on the handle, two curved, wicked talons stretched out from the bulbous bottom. The digital readout went from green to orange. "These claws can sink into any surface. Set and forget. Three o'clock set. Six o'clock forget." She reached out into the casket and pulled out a thumb-sized detonator. "Remote detonators mapped to each bomb. Take these with you."

"Ah, this might be a super dumb question. But what are we doing with these and what are they for?" Natalie asked.

"Soldier, we are going to be deployed behind enemy lines. We are going to make it into the Nagaplex and then deploy these bombs. After that the Nagaplex will be destroyed," said General Katana.

"Do all six of them have to be deployed?" asked Jadyn.

It was on all their minds. Not everyone would survive. *This is suicidal*, thought Ben.

"Yes, because they need to be put at different positions. Each of those positions are structural weaknesses within the Nagaplex," said Mia.

"I'll work that one out with my soldiers," said General Katana. "In battle all plans go out the window. We may need to improvise on positioning."

Andy and Matt had been quiet all this time. Andy reached for one and held it in his hand. "Heavy. It'll slow us down." The left side of the bomb said 10kg/22lb.

"What happens if we group them?" asked Matt.

"If you blow them up all close together?" asked Mia. Matt nodded. She said, "A really concentrated dosage of the Agent Yellow will be sent into one area. What we're aiming to do is inject Agent Yellow in all of the main veins of the Nagaplex. We don't know which one of them is the one that leads to the Nagaplex's heart. So we isolated six possibilities."

Ben felt serious impostor syndrome. The Black Berets should've been in this position with General Katana, not a group of his high school friends with three months of training.

The lights in the cabin bathed them in red. A warning beeped sounded.

"Approaching Nagaplex. T-minus sixty seconds until landing. Coming in hot. Stay strapped in," Julie's voice said over the speakers.

Explosions kaboomed in the sky, causing the G15-Venator to buckle wildly.

Chapter 30

Ace Pilot

The Nagaplex fortified itself in the middle of Australian desert. Ironically, the local place named itself Alice Springs. Alice Sands would have been more appropriate. To get to the Nagaplex, Julie had to fly with full afterburners for one hour since the Nagaplex was a thousand miles away.

Julie piloted the G15-Venator through the red desert that surrounded the Nagaplex for thousands of miles as a hail of projectiles exploded in front of her like fireworks in the night sky. Her hand rattled against the yoke as she pulled up abruptly. Five g-forces squished her mercilessly back into the pilot seat. She hoped Ben and his squad had strapped themselves securely back there.

Alarms blared in her cockpit. Lots of beeping red. She wished she knew the craft as well as she did the F33s.

General Katana's coordinates were suicidal. Behind enemy lines. That meant somehow sneaking in and landing without getting shot.

"Albatross One, this is Eagle Two and Eagle Three," said a voice in her helmet. "We'll try our best to clear a path for you."

The voice crackled in Julie's helmet. Two angular silhouettes of F33-Boomerangs appeared out of the dark like sharks.

"Eagle Two and Three, boy am I glad to see you. I thought I was on my own for a second," said Julie. Her mind worked furiously. She'd studied the 3D models of the Nagaplex for so many years in high school.

The Nagaplex appeared ten miles up ahead like an indistinct murky cloud on the horizon. At fifteen thousand feet high, the Nagaplex looked like a massive black oil stain against the red Australian desert.

"Albatross One, can you share your flight plan?"

Julie closed her eyes. She remembered back in high school studying the 3D model of the Nagaplex and Mister Hackle being so mean about it. Now she understood why. Her life depended on it.

She remembered that the Nagaplex grew into the air like a giant-sized octopus, but instead of suckers the Nagaplex had huge sweeping horns that twisted into the air like cyclones. Nobody knew what those horns did but they were wide and large enough to fit five New York subway trains side-by-side.

Julie opened her eyes and tapped on the map computer. The screen the size of a small tablet. She ensured the coordinates were right.

"Julie," said Mia, entering the cockpit. "There is a safe strip about a mile away from the Nagaplex. You could land there."

"No, Ben and his team would have to go on foot for a mile. They'll be slaughtered. It'd be Naga infestation right there," Julie said, her mind furiously thinking.

"Eagle Two. Eagle Three. I have the flight path. You may download." Julie closed her eyes. Thirty seconds passed and it seemed an eternity. She'd dredged the memories from her time in Mister Hackle's Xenoarchitecture class.

"Acknowledged Albatross One, we have received the flight path. Please confirm that you want to proceed."

"Confirmed," Julie said. She turned to Mia. "Strap in. It's going to get rough."

Up ahead it looked like a computer game. The entire night sky was littered with brilliantly lit projectiles. *Those must be the soldiers from the other capital bases,* Julie thought.

Julie's map display showed the outline of the Nagaplex growing in size. Up ahead she could now see the massive twisting structure that blotted out the entire horizon. In the last five minutes she'd descended from fifteen thousand feet to a thousand feet.

A scream peppered into Julie's headphones as Eagle Two burst into a ball of flame right in front of her. She jerked on the yoke and the G15 screeched as its quadrotors tried to stabilize.

"Albatross One, stick to your flight plan. I've got this," said Eagle Three's voice in her helmet. The tears in Eagle Three's voice couldn't be disguised.

Julie shoved all her shield power to the front shields, leaving the back of the aircraft exposed. It was all in now.

The Nagaplex reared up ahead. The first thing Julie thought was that it resembled nothing human built. It was black like a large octopus with horns in place of suckers. And huge, thousands of feet tall, occupying the entire horizon. It sat over the red desert like a glistening crab.

Black vitriol-like projectiles hurled themselves from slitted organic openings within the Nagaplex and slammed against the G15. Immediately, Julie's shields went from 100% down to 5%. In one hit.

"Shit, shit, shit." Julie's left hand pulled back on the thrusters very delicately, slowing her speed from six hundred miles an hour down to three hundred. The next thing she attempted she'd never even practiced.

"I've got you, Albatross One."

Those were the last words from Eagle Three. Several slits along one of the huge horns of the Nagaplex opened as the G15 roared past. Julie was the first pilot to actually fly over so close to the Nagaplex without getting shot.

The slits emitted a black sludge-like projectile that slammed into Eagle Three. Eagle Three banked and twisted. The F33-Boomerang slid sideways in the air and crashed into the Nagaplex at six hundred miles per hour. A huge burn mark flared across the black skin of the Nagaplex, and the entire structure shuddered.

Julie pushed the thrusters to 'Off' just as another set of projectiles shot at her. She managed to turn the G15 to its side where the bulk of its armor lay, and the impact rocked the aircraft. The sound of metal tearing screeched into Julie's ear as the side panels from the G15 ripped apart and clanged against the Nagaplex.

"Down, down, down. Mayday!" Julie screeched. Her hand refused to give away from holding the yoke even as the g-force caused her to black out. Some part of her was aware of the spiraling G15 as she guided it to land on the only spot that might give them a chance of surviving.

The world spun. Darkness. Wisp of madness. The screaming of Nagas. Julie's dad giving her a hug before he left for the EDF. She remembered the F33 badge her dad dropped into her nine-year-old palm.

Fire and damnation enveloped Julie.

It was painful. It was oh so painful.

ʓ

Strapped to the seat in the passenger cabin in the back of the G15, Ben felt like a toy in the jaw of a rabid dog. His body shook. His vision blurred. A loud *ka-chung* rang in his ears, followed by a large force that punched him in the gut and rendered him breathless. Bright purple anti-crash gel shot out all over the cabin, coating all seven passengers.

Mia's eyes opened wide in shock and she held out her hands to him. He wanted to take her hand but his entire body hurled itself out the back of the G15 as the emergency responses kicked in and their seats ejected them sideways.

Coated in the anti-crash gel, Ben slammed into a wall fifty feet high and slid all the way to the ground. The crash gel left streaks of purple on the wall and a puddle on the floor, but it dissipated the majority of force that would've otherwise killed the occupants.

The G15 screeched to a sliding halt, tilting on its side. The twin cockpit caved in on the right side. One wing tilted at an odd angle.

Six other people lay around the G15 like purple balls of gel as the gel began to melt.

Ben struggled to his feet, wiping off the purple gel. Where was his M18? He found his rifle a few feet away from him with the sticky gel still clinging to its squat barrel. He cleaned the gel and aimed it instantly.

The light from the gun illuminated a crash-landing site stretching over a mile long. The G15's cockpit was only a few feet away from him.

General Katana and Jadyn heaved a huge section of wing that tilted dangerously over the cockpit. It had to be thousands of pounds, but the General and Jadyn shoved it off with a clang.

"Julie!" Ben said, running to the cockpit. He'd seen her hand outside of the cockpit holding onto her helmet.

Julie's gold-blonde hair was plastered with blood. Her neck tilted to the side. Her seatbelt made an X across her torso and it was also caked in blood. A piece of shrapnel jutted through her left forearm, pinning it to the seat's sidearm.

"Ben?" Julie said, her eyes all wide as she glanced about. Confusion covered her face. "We made it." The confusion replaced itself with relief.

Ben grasped her hand. It was cold.

"Julie, stay with me—" He turned around and yelled for help. "This is going to hurt." He got hold of the shrapnel and pulled it out. Quickly, he grabbed the antiseptic foam and the bandage from his backpack. He sprayed her hand with the foam, and then wrapped the bandage around it snugly.

"Here, I'll get her out." Jadyn came and ripped away the overhanging canopy and threw it aside with a clang. Ben didn't even have the strength to push the canopy aside. The big soldier then reached it and scooped Julie out. Ben quickly clicked on the harness buckles to release Julie.

"I never knew you were so handy with a bandage." Julie's eyes stared around at the Nagaplex, noticing the strange glowing symbols underneath the black walls. "It looks beautiful, Ben."

Ben laughed. It came out as a sob. A thousand things came to him. All the things he'd wanted to say to her but forgot. She was one of the few people in his life who encouraged him all the way back then. She'd seen something in him and he'd been a complete scoundrel back then. He'd changed so much. He wanted to show her how much better he'd become.

"Ben, promise me you'll finish the Nagas?" Julie asked. Her eyes closing.

He nodded through the tears in his eyes.

"I've always wanted to fly." Julie's last words were a whisper that hung in the air along with her soul. Her head fell back against the seat, and the helmet she held in her hand thumped to the ground outside of the cockpit.

"Noo!" Ben's scream ricocheted against the walls and went right into the heart of the Nagaplex.

"She's fine," said Jadyn, gripping Ben's shoulder. "She's fine. Just dazed and weak."

Natalie lay at Julie's side. She checked her entire body for any wounds. "She's in shock. She'll recover. You got the wound with the foam."

"Soldier!" General Katana's hand wrapped around the scruff of Ben's neck and ripped him up. "Attention!"

The shock of the command pulled Ben back to his senses. He scrambled to stand next to his squad. Jadyn, Zhi, Natalie, Mia, Matt, and Andy all stood there with purple gel slicking down their wet uniforms.

"Operation King Cobra depends on all of you. We make our way into the hatchery. Leave Julie here. She's our only escape. I hope that thing can still fly. Keep close formation. Hurry. We have the element of surprise and need to make the most of it. Our friends sacrificed their lives for us. We will mourn them after the Nagas are dead." General Katana saluted to Julie's prone but breathing body.

As one, Alpha One Tango saluted too.

The gaping maw of the Nagaplex beckoned them in.

Chapter 31

The Battle of Alice Springs

Forty thousand Earth Defense Force soldiers fought a losing battle against the rush of the Nagas. The soldiers came from each of the four capital bases. They launched their missions as soon as General Katana had given the word during the ambush in Capital Base Oceania. Three other ambushes had occurred in all of the other capital bases. It had been a coordinated pre-emptive strike by the Nagas.

Within an hour of the General's orders, the Earth Defense Force soldiers flew from their respective bases from all around the world and convened in the center of Australia to engage the Nagas in combat.

Each of the four capital bases covered north, east, south, and west directions in order to surround the Nagaplex. Originally planned as a four hundred thousand soldier full frontal assault to 'rattle the teeth of the Nagas,' as the Earth Defense Force broadcasters had said, they were now left to a paltry forty thousand, 90% less, due to the pre-emptive strike launched by the Nagas against each of the capital bases.

Each of the four capital bases fought to defend against some type of giant worm the likes of which they had never seen before. The Naga pre-emptive strike against the capital bases would be cited as the most surprising attack that resulted in the highest toll of any previous military action.

Right then the forty thousand troops stood only ten minutes away from complete annihilation.

Squad Leader Dwayne Jordan arrived from Capital Base Afroasia to the middle of Australia, Alice Springs, in under one hour. The Afroasia platoon was the first to deploy from two badly battered and bruised C10M Super-Titans. The aircraft's engines groaned as it flew to five thousand feet. All ten thousand troops parachuted over a ten-mile area and would navigate their way to a two-mile square coordinate.

That was two hours ago. Now Dwayne surveyed the horizon ahead of him and tried hard to avoid the gnawing fear that snapped its jaws at him, ready to tear at him and spit him out. This was what he'd trained for.

Fighting Nagas. Hand to hand.

He wore his helmet toggled to full-face protection mode. The visor was still up. He liked to get his eyes adjusted to the night naturally before using the optics in his visor.

The dark night covered the land in purple. A squinty pale moon shed the barest of light on the sliver of dead trees that littered the red desert.

A lot of people didn't understand how large Australia was until they landed. The entire middle of Australia was vaster than all the European countries squished together. And all of it was barren.

The only thing that occupied this bareness was the Nagaplex sitting amid the red desert like a black twisted thorn.

Dwayne reached up and snapped his visor down. It clicked and hissed as it pressurized his helmet. Nagas liked to spit acid on soldiers, and that acid ate oxygen and burned through almost anything. The helmets had a specialized disinfectant that would jet out when detecting the Naga venom and clean the helmet. It also provided filtered oxygen. He could walk into noxious fumes with his helmet on.

As soon as Dwayne's visor activated, that fear came right back and snapped its jaws over him. He almost pissed himself.

The visor's night vision illuminated what his eyes couldn't see: the flash of movement, tall swaying still, and then slithering. If it wasn't for his night vision, he wouldn't have spotted them: thousands of Nagas slithered in the sand. They headed right at his men.

Dwarfing the Nagas, the Nagaplex rose like a giant spiked octopus. It was larger than ten pyramids combined and rose thousands of feet into the air. Its tendril-like structure looked like the earth had spat out a cancerous growth.

"Engage on one," Dwayne spoke into his helmet's receiver. "Ten, nine, eight, seven, six, five, four, three, two, one." His squad acknowledged his comms in complete silence. Normally they were a chatty bunch.

Not tonight.

M18 tracer fire lit the air.

Somebody screamed as a Naga crushed them alive.

Dwayne looked up and thought he caught a glimpse of a G15-Venator flying full speed at the Nagaplex. "Godspeed, General Katana."

Chapter 32

Galaxies Collide

The entrance of the Nagaplex consisted of a seven sided heptagonal hole that stretched out wide and high as four humans. A deep darkness beckoned within and a cloying smell oozed out in the form of a purple fog that rolled along the ground. Strange symbols etched within heptagonal tiles that stretched away to either side of Alpha One Tango.

General Katana stood at the entrance. Her face covered in shadow as she turned and looked at them. The two katana's on her back made a zinging sound as she whipped them free.

"Stay close, fire at will," said the general, stepping into the black hole and disappearing within.

"On me. Dial helmets to full. The air might not be safe for us to breathe in there," said Zhi.

Ben's visor hissed down over him. The speakers crackled to life. His breathing sounded too loud in his own ears. Somehow, he felt claustrophobic instead of safe with the visor down.

"Remember your formations. This is what we trained for every single day," said Zhi. "Andy and Matt, you guys stay in the middle. Mia you stay in between them."

Ben's position was always at the front of the formation next to Zhi. Jadyn took up the rear. He could see over all of them and fire above their heads. Natalie took up a position with Jadyn at the rear. Only her job was to cover their rear from flanking maneuvers.

Ben heaved a deep breath. Turned one last time to look at his squad and gave them a brief salute. He was glad Zhi put Mia right in the middle where she would be protected. He was trying not to think about Julie out there alone.

They'd found a mismatched assortment of armor in the G15. They looked like a bunch of recruits on their first day. They couldn't find any armor that fitted Jadyn except for a large helmet. Besides him everyone else sported different sizes of armor all over them.

The slippery floor made treacherous footing. The heptagon tiles began glowed a dim purple and brightened the deeper they went.

General Katana stalked up ahead. Her two shoulder mounted turrets scanned the air in their red laser lights. She looked formidable.

The light bathed Mia in a slight glow. She was the only one who didn't have any armor on. Pearlescent drops of sweat beaded her forehead. She kept licking her lips. Black smudges stretched across her neck and smeared itself on her white collar. Still, there appeared a curiosity in the way she looked about. As if she'd dreamed of coming here.

The strange heptagonal tunnel curved right. The more they moved in the thicker the air became. Each time they went around a bend - a blind corner - General Katana signalled for them to halt and she would clear the point before allowing them to move on.

At one particular point the general called to a halt quite abruptly. Ben's hands shook where he held the M18's grip.

A huge snakeskin the size of a bus stretched the length of the tunnel and disappeared under purple fog. It looked like the corpse of a Naga. The snakeskin resembled a net used to capture sharks. General Katana bent down and pulled on the net removing a glistening golden naga scale. The scale fitted across her entire hand. She handed it to Mia.

Everyone's adrenaline spiked. If something moved right then it would've be riddled with bullets.

"Let's go," said Zhi.

Ben shook himself. His eyes on the snakeskin so much so that he didn't see

General Katana disappear further ahead. Stay focussed, he told himself.

They crept up further ahead. The tunnel went upward and widened considerably. At the top of the slope the tunnel branched out into five directions. Two tunnels went down and left and two tunnels went down and right. One tunnel went up through the middle.

A faint sound trickled up from the middle tunnel. General Katana halted. Her head tilted slightly as she listened. She strode forward but signalled them to either side, spread out. As if wanting to keep them away from the damage of a Naga's venom spit attack.

The tunnel eventually opened out and widened into a heptagonal chamber. The light brightened considerably. A red hue came from a heptagonal dome that glowed brightly. They appeared to be in the heart of a cavern that stretched out all around them. The temperature also rose considerably, suddenly. It was very hot and Ben sweated beneath his armor.

A tall sinuous platform rose from the middle of the floor and stretched almost all the way to the dome. It looked to be some type of statue or carving.

General Katana hissed. Her sword blades pointed at the statue and her shoulder turrets jerked upright making a high whistling sound. But their lasers couldn't seem to catch on the target.

What Ben saw next made him whimper.

The tall sinuous platform twisted to face them. A red giant sized Naga uncoiled itself and the entire ground floor shifted as it did so. The elaborate red tiles on the floor belonged to its never ending sinuous body that coiled underneath it. A hood flared into the air. Blue eyes, so intelligent, stared at them.

Ben felt the fear shake him. From feeling hot he suddenly went cold. His neck constricted. Memories of his childhood suffused him. In particulate a nightmarish memory ten years ago in Central Park. He knew those blue eyes.

"Imperator Kaali," said General Katana. "I've come to finish what I started."

Hearing General Katana's voice unfroze Ben.

"It's a pity you were not suited for our bracelet," said Imperator Kaali. "You would have made a fine breeder. Nagas prize courage above all else." When the Naga spoke its forked tongue sliced into the air. Its head moved side to side in an oddly hypnotic movement.

"Already we have decimated your frontal assault forces. How pitiably weak you humans are," said Imperator Kaali. "But yes, you are always an odd surprise, Katana. You came through the one entrance we could not protect. And look at you, you have lost all of your humanity. You look more like a robot than a human."

General Katana walked sideways, heading to the left of the huge towering serpent in front of all of them. The serpent's hood trailed her. Showing its back to Ben's squad.

Jadyn nodded at Zhi. Should he fire? Zhi vehemently shook her head.

"Do you see those archways? When the general attacks that's where we go," Zhi's voice came into Ben's helmet. "Do not move before. Make sure that snake is fully engaged. It could kill us all with a swipe of its tail."

The seven sided archways looked like sunken eye pits. Slimy and webby things went from their tops down to the bottom. Beyond the archways strange bulbous things hung from the ceiling. The stench of rot filled the air.

"The hatchery," said Mia, her voice quivering with fear and anticipation. "We're so close."

General Katana skidded to the side and somersaulted as Imperator Kaali's hood flared like a whip into the air. His jaws snapped revealing teeth the size of a person and spitting blistering poison that slammed into the spot General Katana just stood on. The entire ground blistered revealing a hole that showed the level below.

General Katana already evaded. She knelt on one knee with the other leg stretch out. Her shoulder turrets fired. Miniature sidewinder missiles flew out and twirled into the air. They exploded before reaching Imperator Kaali filling the air with a ringing sound.

For a half second the huge Naga trembled.

"Now!" shouted Zhi. She dashed across the dome.

But a resounding crash echoed all around them and Imperator Kaali's thick coils blocked their exit. Andy and Matt peeled away to the side and fired their M18's. Their aims twin precisions of engineering. Right in the middle of the Naga's head where the projectiles would stand the chance to do most damage. The Naga rounds punctured the air with its sonic whine. A few bullets scorched the side of the Naga's hood.

Ben, Jadyn, Natalie, and Zhi ran in formation. Ben didn't realize his two friends peeled to the side until the very last moment.

Andy and Matt's spontaneous decision attracted the attention of Imperator Kaali which gave the squad members of Alpha One Tango the chance they required to flee.

Imperator Kaali's tail fanned into the air and split into three sharp blades. Projectiles whizzed into the air. So many of them it appeared like a hive of mosquitoes bearing knives. The sharp projectiles shredded through Andy and Matt like they were cheese. Their bodies instantly turning into shredded human and collapsed to the ground like minced beef.

At this opportune moment General Katana ran forward. Her shoulder turrets firing in the air. Her metallic legs and torso enabled her to withstand enormous amounts of force. Her upper torso connected to her metallic legs enabled her to swivel around three hundred sixty degrees as Imperator Kaali's tail whipped at her.

The general's missiles exploded in front of the naga's hood causing it momentarily confusion. General Katana leaped into the air, her robotic legs pistoning, the pneumatic recoil pushing her way beyond the normal leaping ability of a human. She hovered behind Imperator Kaali's head and her hands shot out holding out her katana blades. She stabbed into the back of the snake's head and hung on with dear life as her katana blades cut down two vertical lines at the back of the snake's hood.

Imperator Kaali screamed and twisted his head blindly. General Katana held on until the very last moment when he caught her in a whiplash and sent her body careening against the top of the dome. Her body bounced with such force that it escaped another whiplash straight after.

General Katana thudded to the ground and rolled. Ben held his breath thinking she was dead.

She turned to look at them. "Go!"

Imperator Kaali whipped his neck around the general. His snakelike body wrapping her up in bands of scales. Huge black wings shot out from Imperator Kaali's shoulders. With a single whip of his wings he broke through the dome taking the general with him.

"Let's go!" Zhi's voice screamed into Ben's helmet.

All he could see was the limp form of General Katana in the huge wings of Imperator Kaali and thousands of shards of glass crashing towards them.

Chapter 33

Princess Saar

The scream came from behind the squad members of Alpha One Tango. They almost stopped to turn but Zhi ordered them to keep going.

The Naga hatchery spread around Ben like an alien forest, so large and vast. The egg sacs dangled from the top of the ceiling from vast stalactites. It felt to all of them that they'd entered an alien planet. Purple fog roiled from the ground. Each of their steps made a mushy *squish* noise.

"It had damn wings," Natalie kept saying and repeating in her helmet.

"Andy and Matt," said Jadyn. "They were vaporized..."

Ben's boots squelched into a puddle of goop. He was trying hard not to think of his friends. Not now. He needed to stay frosty.

"Shut up and stay frosty," Zhi commanded into the squad channel. Immediately, Jadyn and Natalie fell silent. "We'll mourn them when we get out of here."

It reminded Ben of the time his dad took him to the Redwood Forest in California. Ben, Mia, her mom, and his dad formed a ring by holding hands and the only went halfway around the base of the redwood tree. Each of those stalactites jutting down from the ceiling was just as wide.

Each of the egg sacs stood taller than twenty feet and wider than a person. They hung down from their striated thick webbing. The webbing clasped to the bottom of the bulging egg sacs where pearlescent drops glistened and fell. A thick cloying sweet smell filled the air.

"Jesus," said Jadyn. "It's moving."

Ben raised his M18 and sighted.

One of the egg sacs quivered. A purple vein pulsed. The light from Ben's M18 showed the outline of a Naga hatchling. A hatchling the size of a damn car.

"Prime the Agent Yellow," Zhi ordered. "This place looks to be the size of a football stadium. We'll plant them equidistantly divided into six."

Mia nodded. "Yes, that's right. But... we imagined the eggs would be on the ground. Not up so high."

"Does it matter?" asked Zhi.

"Yes, it shoots out a liquid. The Agent Yellow. We need to plant the bombs upside down." She was about to say something else but her mouth went shut.

"Very well," said Zhi.

Ben was too in awe to even remotely think what the biological contaminant would do to him.

"Go and be careful. There could be other Nagas lying in ambush," said Zhi. "Rendezvous back here. You have five minutes. Mia, stay with me. We'll plant our bomb right here."

Ben, Natalie, Jadyn, and Zhi met eyes. They nodded. So many things flashed through Ben's mind. Nothing came out of his mouth. He just wanted to thank them. He would be dead soon. Much better people than him had already died.

This was what they'd done during all those orientation and map reading exercises. Now he understood. It was impossible to pick out a landmark in this crepuscular jungle of creepy things. Everywhere Ben looked he thought a Naga would explode from an egg sac and kill him. The farther he went into the hatchery, the higher the purple fog rose. Until it reached just under his nose.

He'd marked position on his M18's small scanner. It was a crappy monochrome black and green scanner. But it was built tough and was super reliable. He squinted at it as he marked his turns. Half a mile east, then half a mile west. He'd climbed a hundred meters. All the while a creeping fear began to take hold of him.

"Stay calm," he spoke into his helmet. He didn't even realize his words had a calming effect on the rest of his squad, who were right then doing the same thing he was doing.

Zhi wanted the Agent Yellow bombs spread equidistantly. Ben was putting his bomb in the farthest section.

Eventually, he found his spot. He knelt on the ground, grabbed the bomb from his backpack shell. He slammed the heavy bulbous body down into the ground like Mia showed them and then twisted up at the handle. Two curved dagger-like hands emerged from the sides. As they hit the ground they twisted.

"Set and forget," he said to himself.

The first twist was for 3 o'clock. Set. Breathing deeply. He kept looking at the huge egg sacs above his head that wobbled. He twisted the bomb's handle to 6 o'clock. Forget. The motor whirred and burrowed itself deeply into the wet ground. The entire kettlebell-shaped bomb disappeared in the purple fog.

He'd been on his knees the entire time doing that. Now he stood and the ground rumbled beneath him. He tottered to his feet and nearly fell. Grabbing his M18, he stared at its scanner, reversing its route. He needed to get back to the rendezvous point.

All around him was purple fog. Above him endless rows of egg sacs dangled down. He shoved them out of his mind and followed the coordinates he'd set, hoping he wasn't going to get lost.

Ben stumbled out of the purple fog, terrified he'd gotten lost, when he spotted Zhi and Mia talking.

"Jadyn? Natalie?" Ben asked.

"Shiz, thought I got lost," came a voice behind him. A towering sweaty-faced Jadyn stumbled toward them. His breath rushing. He doubled over, dry-heaving.

They waited a tense minute. Ben was deathly afraid Zhi would make him go find Natalie when their last squad mate came out of the purple fog.

Natalie's lower lip trembled. She held out her detonator. It was small, designed to fit ergonomically within the palm of a hand. It had a single button that blinked blue. It would turn red when activated.

They each had a detonator.

"Ready?" Zhi said.

Zhi spoke too soon.

A Naga slithered out from the fog and stared at them. Its pale gray eyes blinked suddenly. It didn't have any scales, Ben realized. Pale skin showed where there should've been scales. It was much smaller than the Nagas they had all seen. It was about the size of a large anaconda. With an unusually large head thrice the size of its body.

Mia spoke. "Are you the hatch keeper?"

Four M18's pointed their nozzles at the Naga.

"I'm not the hatch keeper, you sniveling puss bag," said the Naga. It began to slither back slightly.

"Fire!" Zhi ordered.

Ben pressed his trigger. The M18 buckled in his hands like a bronco as the powerful slugs shot out.

The Naga screeched and whipped its head back. Bullets flayed open skin, revealing tendons and ligaments. Purple blood oozed from the wounds.

"Stop!" a commanding voice shouted.

A powerful force ripped the M18s out from their hands. Ben's gun flew into the air and hovered just near the injured white Naga.

Ben's eyes bulged. Psychokinesis? How was that even possible?

The white Naga sobbed. Its cries sounded like the scream of a witch. A young girl stepped out from the fog and laid her hands against the Nagas ripped torso and bleeding underbelly. The skin that had been torn and shredded and oozing purple blood stitched itself back together.

Ben realized he couldn't move. He was rooted to the spot. He had never seen such a beautiful person in his entire life.

"Vhaldie, you will survive," she said.

"Saar, your father—"

"I know," said the young woman. The white snake slumped as if underneath a sleeping spell and didn't stir.

The young woman turned to face them. There was something utterly alien about her. It was her eyes that captured Ben's attention. They looked exactly like a serpent's. Except, somehow, they were beautiful on her face. A face with elongated jaws, tilted eyes, small ears. She did not walk; she sashayed.

"You are The Chosen," the lady said, pointing toward the squad members of Alpha One Tango. "Yet you come here with violence. Why?"

"Put your hands in the air and get down on your knees," said Zhi. Her voice trailed into silence as she realized she couldn't even move. Her eyes strained downward to where her handgun sat inside the holster on her hip.

The young lady tilted her head as if examining something. She didn't even acknowledge Zhi's outburst.

It was Mia who said the words that blew Ben's mind. Mia said, "I mean you no harm. May I step closer to see you?"

The young woman nodded.

Mia was freed somehow and then they all were, Ben realized. He could move. But he didn't dare.

Mia walked toward the young lady. Even if they could shoot, they would now risk shooting Mia.

Wonderment and curiosity filled Mia's tone. She walked around the young lady, staring at her up and down as if she was some experiment in Mia's lab. Eventually Mia stopped.

Mia held out her hand. "Do you have a name?"

"I am Princess Saar," the young lady said. A sibilant hiss echoed around the vowels.

Princess? Ben found himself whispering her name, "Saar," under his breath. What a beautiful name. His eyes widened as he recollected his meeting with the girl - it hadn't been a hallucination because of all the drugs in his system. She was real. He wanted to reach out to her. But Mia had beaten him to it.

"Saar, I am Mia. I do not wish you harm."

Saar reached out tentatively and touched Mia's hand. As if the concept of a handshake was something alien to her. Mia smiled. She reached out and held Saar's hand and then she said. "This is how we handshake." She mimed it using her own hands. "It is a gesture of welcoming and friendship."

Saar smiled. Her hand reached out and grasped Mia's.

Mia screamed. "Ouch!"

Saar let go. Her eyes widening in shock.

Jadyn dashed forward and tackled Mia to safety.

Zhi reached for her holster and grabbed her H5 Boxer and pulled the trigger. That gun was a .7 caliber and it was made to take out holes in tanks and Nagas. The supersonic bullet shot out with a bang.

A millionth of a millionth of a second and Saar stood there holding the bullet in her hand. An inquisitive look on her face.

"What is—"

"Detonate!" Zhi shouted and pressed her detonator.

Ben, Zhi, and Jadyn all pressed their detonator's simultaneously.

Saar, sensing something, looked about wildly. Her eyes narrowed suddenly. "Liar!" she screamed at Mia.

The stench came first. It smelled like somebody dying had pooped. Ben struggled not to vomit. But the shock that rattled him was the effect the Agent Yellow had on Saar.

A fine yellow mist, the Agent Yellow, now fought savagely against the purple fog. Where the yellow mist touched the purple, the ground and undergrowth blackened and withered. The yellow mist was slowly rising toward the egg sacs.

"Nooo!" Saar screamed as the yellow mist engulfed her. Her skin turned translucent, revealing scales beneath the beautiful fairness. Her jaws widened beyond what was normal in a human. She transformed grotesquely, her body shifting, melting, tendons knotting and popping until a huge snake writhed there. It was a golden snake. A magnificent and beautiful golden snake.

It turned and fled.

The Nagaplex trembled beneath them. Egg sacs shook as the Agent Yellow ate into them. A booming sound filled with fear and outrage rent the air.

"Go!" Zhi screamed.

Chapter 34

Ultimate Sacrifice

General Katana felt like her head had been slammed through a dozen ten-foot-thick walls over and over again. Everything rang. Her upgraded limbs blared alarms saying, "Threshold criticality surpassed." Her lower back arched with pain as she let out a scream.

In the hold of the Naga, she thought she would be squeezed to death. The first thing she could see was those red scales all around her body, wrapping across her back and her front. Only her hands were up, clutching uselessly at the scales. Her katana blades long gone.

She looked up to see the rushing dome come crumbling down as Imperator Kaali burst through it. The tight scales wrapped around her uncoiled and flung her. She careened against a wall and skimmed the ground several times before coming to a halt.

General Katana crawled to her feet. She unsheathed her small vibro blade and slammed it on the ground and used its leverage to pull herself up.

The light in this chamber glowed yellow. A large reclining seat sat in the middle, made out of golden stones in the shape of a many-headed serpent. She started for a moment, thinking it was a real Naga. It appeared to be some type of controller seat.

That realization only made sense because all around her there appeared several holographic projections. Each one showed a different aspect of what was what happening outside.

Imperator Kaali eyed the holographic projections. His entire being mesmerized by what it was showing. It was as if her presence was just that of an ant. A pool of Naga blood oozed down his hood and splashed on the ground. Purple blood. His huge jaws hung open and his forked tongue dangled down.

"What did you mean about the bracelet?" asked General Katana.

Imperator Kali turned and gave off the effect of stone becoming fluid. General Katana found herself stepping back. The huge Naga was over fifty feet tall and only twenty feet away. He could cover that distance ten times faster than she could.

"Annoying human," said Imperator Kaali. "You know not the forces you meddle against. Stupid foolish humans. It's your lifespan. It makes you shortsighted." The giant snake slithered down, its head snaking left and right as it neared her. "It's time for you to die."

"Why wasn't I suited for the bracelet?" asked General Katana, sliding against the wall. There were two more of those huge reclining seats made out of the golden stone. Was that where they controlled the Nagaplex from?

"The bracelets are for The Chosen. You are not." He was halfway across the room. He slithered to the left to avoid the huge crater he had made where the dome had once been. Glass scrunched beneath his impenetrable scales like he was some type of mining machine. He didn't let his bleeding head slow him down. But General Katana could tell the blood loss affected him. There was a slight wooziness to his movements.

"What will The Chosen do?" she asked.

Imperator Kaali stopped suddenly. He jerked his huge head upward. It approximated such a human-like gesture she was almost convinced he was a man inside a snake.

"You humans never figured it out?" His body rumbled with laughter. "They are to be mates for our younglings."

"Mates? As in you think we can mate with your kind and have children?" His answer dumfounded General Katana. How could that even be possible? The Nagas and humans were two distinct species.

"You're dying, you should not have come back. It's a pity you were not born a

Naga. Your spirit is wasted on the human species," said Imperator Kaali. He attacked.

The massive Naga corkscrewed right at her. She'd made herself a diminutive target. Hunkering down on her one knee, with her one hand holding her weight, she looked up at him like she was a dying morsel.

For a terrifying moment all she could feel was the entirety of her fear. A cold searing thing as she stared at what had scared human beings since they were Neanderthals: being eaten alive.

Snake jaws the size of cars snapped open. Glistening, poisonous fangs ripped at the air. The stench of rotten dead flesh assailed General Katana in her final moments.

But she did not evade. Instead she launched herself forward with the remaining power in her bionic legs. The pistoning motion shuddered her body and the pneumatic recoil tore through her already torn up body. Alarms blared in her vision. She ignored it all.

General Katana flew into the gaping jaws of death. Fangs snapped at her. Hot breath. Acid. Poison. It all engulfed her. She screamed as the poison melted her alive. Turning her into molten slag of bits of bone and machinery.

But not before General Katana bit into the self-activation button at the back of her tongue. Felt its ashy taste in her mouth as the detonator flared to life and then a blooming hotness filled her soul.

A warm blooming hotness that wiped out her pain.

Her last thoughts were of her sister, Zhi. She dreamed they were children and playing in the garden again. And all was well.

𝔊

Imperator Kaali's eyes bulged as his jaws engulfed the General completely, swallowing her whole. The millions of incisors lining his multiple inner jaws felt a sudden heat where they should have just met flesh. A searing heat cascaded right up into Kaali's brain. Oxygen sucked itself from his lungs in a single pull. He tried to open his jaws but they were singed shut.

The giant Naga's head flared its hood in the air and then exploded in globules of scales, flesh, teeth, eyes, throat, and brain chunks. The entire Naga's body held itself up for a long moment. The decapitated serpent fountained purple blood all over the room.

The leader of the Naga's occupation on Earth for the last ten years ever since that fateful Invasion Day lay dead, his body slammed to the ground.

What had been the most terrifying monster of all time now looked like an ancient fossil. Strangely, the carcass appeared to age and only left bones

Chapter 35

Nagaplex Rise

The Nagaplex trembled, heaved, and buckled. An earthquake shook the entire area. For ten years the Nagaplex had burrowed its tentacles deep within the earth. Its long tentacles were giant-sized tunnels that stretched all the way down into the Earth's core. On the surface the octopus-shaped structure stopped growing after it occupied a sixty-two-mile radius.

Inside the Nagaplex, the Agent Yellow bombs detonated ten minutes after the squad activated their detonators. Alpha One Tango could never work out why it took the detonation so long, but the delay saved all their lives.

♌

Ben couldn't believe his eyes.

"Shoot, is that really happening?" Jadyn said.

"It's flying? No way," said Natalie.

Only Zhi kept quiet. She stared unblinkingly at the sight outside.

"We suspected something like that," said Mia.

Zhi turned to Mia. "How much did the SDF really know? Who was that girl?"

"Soon, I'll tell you everything," Mia answered.

They stood in the shuddering G15-Venator that somehow Julie had managed to pilot out from the Nagaplex. Its turbines kept making choking sounds and it flew at a tilted angle.

The Nagaplex resembled a giant many-headed snake as it tore its tentacles out from the earth. Clods of earth the size of entire houses flew into the air. Bits of earth rained down on the G15, causing it to dip. Several F33-Boomerangs flew through the air and shot out twisting missiles that exploded against the Nagaplex.

The Nagaplex roared in pain. The F33s looked like small flies against a kraken. The Nagaplex's many limbs spread out in the air like a giant jellyfish. Crackling lightning came from those tentacles. A pulsing energy filled the area. The Nagaplex left a hole in the earth so large it looked as if the planet's heart had been ripped out.

"Is it alive?" Ben asked.

"Yes." Mia nodded.

"Where is it going?" asked Natalie.

"To space," answered Mia.

"Something bad is going to happen," said Jadyn. "We need to get out of here."

"Julie is trying her best," said Ben.

They weren't the only ones in the air. Several other G15s trailed behind them. A C10M Super-Titan began to take off from the ground. A group of soldiers too late to make it to the Titan were left behind. Stranded.

Lots of dead Earth Defense Force soldiers and Nagas littered the battlefield.

"Did the bombs work?" Ben asked Mia.

"Yes, they worked," she replied. Mia suddenly bolted to the cockpit and shouted at Julie. "You need to full throttle it. Now!"

The Nagaplex's many long tentacles twitched and lifted into the air. The entire structure now floated in the air. It was the heaviest structure on Earth by a margin of ten. And it just floated there. Naga technology at its best.

A whirring sound filled the air. A crackling of energy and light emitted at the tips of the Nagaplex's tentacles. Those tentacles spread out in star-shaped pattern and then pushed down. Electricity and thunder filled the sky. A Boom! ignited from beneath the ground of the Nagaplex, and a massive explosion mushroomed into the air.

Ben shouted as the gust of searing heat slammed into the G15, spinning it around like a toy.

That's when Julie managed to activate the quadcopter's afterburners.

The G15-Venator shot forward on a mixture of afterburners and the force from the Nagaplex blast.

The Nagaplex blinked and shot forward, up past the inky clouds, illuminated in a purple coruscating light, and then it shot into space.

Chapter 36

Temporary Antidote

Mia knew they had to act quickly. She'd learned so much in a single night. More than all the years of research she'd done on the Nagas.

There was so much to process. She couldn't wait to get back to her labs. What would the Chief think?

"Base up ahead. It's going be a rough landing, grab on to something," said Julie's voice over the speakers of the G15.

Mia held on to the ragged netting by the side of the wide doorway. Around her stood Ben, Jadyn, Natalie, and Zhi. They looked like they had been through hell. They kept coughing. Sweat beaded their foreheads.

Zhi hadn't said more than three words since the mission.

Outside the sky began to brighten. It was early morning.

Time was of the essence.

When the G15 landed, Mia was the first one to throw open the door. She surprised everyone as she dashed down the ramp. She turned around and held up both her hands. "Don't get out. Stay there!"

A very battered and bruised Chief Admiral Evelyn Wilson came up the ramp just as Mia went down. She handed Mia a box with six green vials.

"You and your friends will be the test subjects for this antidote," said the Chief.

Mia grabbed the box of vials and thudded back into the G15.

Ben, Jadyn, Julie, Natalie, and Zhi's eyes met hers questioningly.

Mia said, "You've been exposed to Agent Yellow. It's lethal to humans. It was meant to be a one-way mission. This antidote was prepared only recently. If you do not take it you will die because your insides will melt."

A badly bandaged but alive Chief Admiral Evelyn Wilson added, "The full treatment will need to be done at the space station. You will be coming with us."

"You've got to be joking," said Natalie, slumping down. "That was the most fun I've had in a long time."

Ben laughed. They all laughed and hugged each other.

Julie, Mia, and the Chief eyed each other.

Mia quickly injected each of her friends with the green antidote. She injected herself too.

"Alpha One Tango, you're coming to space," said the Chief. "This isn't over yet."

Chapter 37

A Colossal Decision

The International Space Station Space Defense Force, ISS-SDF as the locals called it, twinkled with activity. It stretched up ten thousand feet high and over five miles long. The space dock's ramp looked out into the east side of space. Several spacecraft carriers hummed with life as they prepared launch.

This was home to sixty-one thousand of the most elite. Handpicked from the elite of the EDF. The cream of the cream of the crop. The best from the Earth Defense Forces were sent to the Space Defense Force on a regular basis.

From a huge window that stretched out from the briefing center in Strategic Space Command, at the lowest level of the central hub, Chief Admiral Evelyn Wilson put her hands against the black desk and stared at her leadership team.

Behind the Chief, Earth appeared the size of a basketball.

To the left of the ISS-SDF, a glittering Naga wormhole stretched out like an oval eye in space. The gateway stood a thousand kilometers away.

Moments ago she'd seen a sight she didn't think possible: the Nagaplex had flown through the wormhole.

"Our scientists estimate the wormhole will remain active for sixty minutes," said Admiral Vince Farragut, Head of Strategic Command. "After that we will not be able to get through."

Evelyn felt an itch on her back as if the Naga wormhole stared at her. Across from her a huge display showed her the space dock where the space fighter carrier,

Nox-Infernum, prepared itself. The black offensive class carrier looked menacing with its jagged profile and long arcing fins. Weapon bays bristled from its belly to its top. Its huge thrusters still glowed with the heat from its recent test flight. Three large umbilical cords snaked out from the walls of the space dock into the *Nox-Infernum*. Four huge jet bridges were filled with the marching steps of a hundred star fighter pilots, cargo handlers, fighter directors, and a whole lot of others.

"How was Nox's test flight?" Evelyn asked, going back to the black table and sitting down. *Nox-Infernum* meant 'fiery night' and she had named it herself. She would bring a fiery night to the Nagas.

The leaders of the Space Defense Force, Evelyn's four admirals, sat around the table. Admiral Dewey Porter, head of the armed wing, responsible for the SDF's equivalent of the Air Force, cleared his throat.

"Test pass rate of forty nine percent. Still issues with weapon systems, life support, and the anti-gravity systems," he answered. "We are fully working on the problem with our scientist colleagues." Here he indicated the pale, slight woman to his left.

Admiral Sophia Jones, head of the scientists within the Space Defense Force, nodded. "Progress is being made. But the deadlines are killing my people. Some have had no rest. We have started to use the EDF's adrenaline jabs to keep them awake. Needless to say this is dangerous territory."

"I understand," said Evelyn. "But I have only sixty minutes to take the *Nox-Infernum* right through the Naga wormhole."

The doors opened just then and Special Projects Lead Scientist Mia Johnson-Patel strode in with General Katana. Only, it wasn't General Katana but somebody who looked exactly like her. It was startling and Evelyn, who wasn't one to be at a loss for words, just stared.

"Chief Admiral, this is Zhi Bugeisha. General Katana's younger sister. We've been talking and we'd like to propose an idea," said Mia.

The four admirals turned and regarded the two newcomers with frank appraisal. While everyone in the Space Defense

Force knew of the tales of General Katana and held her in awe, none of them knew the six kids who'd changed the course of the war down on Earth.

But the Chief Admiral did.

"Go on," said Evelyn.

Zhi Bugeisha bowed at the Chief. It was odd how eerily similar her mannerisms were to the elder Katana. Evelyn did remember, long ago, that a young woman named Onna Bugeisha had been recruited. But after her heroics displayed in battle, she'd become General Katana: the very emblem and spirit of the Earth Defense Force.

"General Katana gave me these instructions. When the wormhole reopened, she didn't want just the *Nox-Infernum* to go through. She wanted you to send the entire space station through the wormhole—"

The four admirals spoke at once.

"Craziness!"

"You've got to be joking?"

"We have no idea what's on the other side."

The idea floored the Chief Admiral.

"Silence!" Evelyn shouted. She looked at Mia. "Is it possible?"

Mia nodded. "It will take fifty-nine minutes and thirty seconds. I've done the calculations and retrofitted the thrusters."

"We can't make such a colossal decision in thirty seconds," said Admiral Sophia Jones.

"This is absurd," said Admiral Vince Farragut.

That was the problem with her admirals, the chief thought. They lacked the vision of General Katana.

"I've already made my decision," said Chief Admiral Evelyn Wilson. "Move the ISS-SDF into the Naga wormhole."

Mia and Zhi collapsed into two seats by the side of the huge table. They had spent all the time since their arrival working on the idea.

All four of the admirals stood up. They began to shout and gesture.

Chief Admiral Evelyn Wilson stared at the four leaders whom she'd spent the last ten years with. God, what she would do to have General Katana sitting at her table. That loss had cut Evelyn like a blade to the heart. She felt untethered without her EDF counterpart. She didn't know how much she'd relied on Katana until now. Did Katana suffer the same indecisions?

"You will obey or you will be stripped of your command," said Chief Admiral Evelyn Wilson. The last thing she needed was to quell a mutiny.

Her four admiral's revealed different emotions. Emily looked shocked. Dewey merely shrugged. Sophia frowned and scratched her chin. Vince smiled.

Vince said, "About time we took it to the snakes."

"I don't like it. We are going in completely blind," said Emily.

"My pilots are going to pilot that damn thing. They sure as hell need to know," said Dewey.

"We are all in the dark," said Chief Admiral Evelyn Wilson. She held up her hand to forestall her admiral's protests. "Can't you see the benefit? We'll have the Mothership with us. The ISS-SDF is a fully enclosed ecosystem. It was originally designed for colonization and retrofitted for military."

Silence filled the room. Never did any of them think it would come to this.

"God help us all," said Sophia.

Chapter 38

The Snakey Way

Sombrero Galaxy
1 March 2077
17:00

The stars of the disc-shaped Sombrero Galaxy spread out as far as the eye could see. The galaxy stretched out forty nine thousand light-years wide. Right at the edge of this galaxy, two suns floated in the middle of this particular solar system. This solar system had been named Snakey Way by the Space Defense Force.

A string of planets rotated around the twin suns of the Snakey Way solar system. Red, green, blue, yellow, and purple. Mia pointed to Nagaloka, the Nagas' home planet. It orbited the twin suns one hundred million miles away and was the closest planet to them.

"That's the planet the Nagaplex disappeared in," Mia said. Her finger left a smudge on the thick windows that edged one of the walkways in SDF University.

"Thirty one million light-years from Earth," Ben whispered to himself, still not quite believing it. A glittering blue and gold coruscating nebula glimmered in the distance. He wore a patient's blue gown and held on to a thick steel intravenous pole. His right fist shook.

The smaller, scarred hand next to his belonged to Zhi. They both held on to the same pole. Each of them connected to their own IV bags that bulged from the hooks.

Jadyn sat on one of the flat black couches with his legs dangling out from the blue hospital gown. He made the gown look like a mini skirt. His dark legs were covered in yellow splotches. He'd lost so much weight he appeared gaunt. Dark bags circled his eyes.

Ben didn't want to look at himself in the mirror. He'd aged. There was white in his hair. They were all severely malnourished and they all had the same yellow splotches on their legs. That's what happened when you got exposed to Agent Yellow. You got sick.

"When are we going?" Zhi asked. Her hollowed cheeks gave her a feverish glow. It made her seem even more intense than normal, if that was even possible. It was so cold aboard the ISS-SDF. Zhi's eyes were colder.

"Yeah, one week is enough. I mean I need to get out there. I'm going crazy," said Natalie. Strangely out of everyone she appeared to be in the best condition.

"The Planetfall Troopers will be deployed on Nagaloka. It's going to be the largest operation in the history of SDF. I've been so busy making adjustments to the SDF's scanning algorithms. It's unbelievable what it can do now—"

Zhi's thin hand reached out and grabbed Mia's lapel. It brought the scientist to a stop.

"We aren't getting better. Your antidote is not working. You promised us treatment. You said the ISS-SDF would cure us."

"We knew it was going to be bad for humans. We just didn't know it was going to be this bad—"

"You knew and you didn't tell us?" said Ben.

"I tried to tell you, Ben. It was all going crazy." Mia felt the heavy gazes of her friend. She wrung her hands. "Don't you understand it was the end of the human race? We had to do something."

"I'm not going to die in a hospital bed thirty-one million light-years from my damn home," said Zhi. She let go of Mia's lapels. "Who made Agent Yellow?"

"I did."

"Then you need to make the cure," Zhi said. "Yesterday."

Mia swallowed. "I'm working on other—"

"General Katana died to save us. It was Alpha One Tango that put those bombs there. It was Alpha One Tango that got us where we are today. Where the heck do you think the human race would've been without us?" As Zhi spoke the squad members of Alpha One Tango—Jadyn, Natalie, and Ben—gathered behind her. If anything their confinement in the hospital bound them even tighter.

"Hey, when you say it like that, we're heroes, right?" said Natalie. Her pale wispy red hair peppered itself sparsely across her head. Strands of it stuck on the shoulder of her hospital gown.

"It's the military industrial complex," said Mia. "You're only as good as your last game. You guys were trained for Earth. And now you're sick…"

"Then why the heck did the Chief bring us here?" asked Jadyn. "Could've died watching the Superbowl."

"Matt and Andy died to save us," said Ben. "We gave up our lives for this. With all that neuro accelerant crap and those growth hormones. Look at me, Mia. Look at me!" He tottered on his feet. Ben should have been eighteen. But the growth hormones had aged them ten years. "I'm thirty," the words came out in a whisper.

"It wasn't just me," said Mia. "It's not my fault." Tears filled her eyes.

367

"Mia, if you created Agent Yellow you could find a cure for it. There isn't anyone else smarter than you in this damn universe," said Natalie.

"Okay," Mia said, nodding her head. "There may be a way. But it's…going to have ramifications."

"You have a week left before our organs start to break down." Zhi turned the IV pole away and together, she and Ben began to painfully walk back to the two-seater cart that would drive them back to the hospital.

"I will," Mia promised, as she watched her friends amble back as if they were old people. She had an idea. It involved using the red Naga she'd killed in her lab. Well, its DNA, to be precise.

She didn't know how she was going to find the time. Chief Admiral Evelyn Wilson had put her in charge of the urgent work of modifying the sensor algorithms. They operated under the assumption that the ISS-SDF was in imminent danger of being attacked. Without an improved sensor algorithm it would be like flying without a map. Mia needed major breakthroughs.

The Planetfall Troopers would launch themselves into Nagaloka in one week's time.

A Quick Favor...

If you enjoyed this book, please take a moment to write a short review so other readers can enjoy it, too.

Thanks so much!
D.P.Oberon

Grab a free book!

D.P. Oberon is storming up the Amazon charts. As an up and coming author we are giving out his books for free to show our gratitude to the fans who love the Naga Invasion series.

www.dpoberon.com
https://www.dpoberon.com/paperbackoffer.html

VISIT